Night Beast

"Hypnotic and elegant, *Night Beast* built to a resonance that resounds in me still. These stories are unforgettable, full of longing and hunger and alert tenderness. Finishing the collection was like waking from a night of disquieting and luminous dreams. I did not want this book to end." —ANNA NOYES, author of *Goodnight, Beautiful Women*

"So many of the characters in Ruth Joffre's stories are, literally and figuratively, sleepwalking through 'some dark and frightful dream that our minds had conjured,' and it's a testament to Joffre's meticulous and abundant talent that she can guide the reader through these constrained and inhospitable spaces. No matter how dark the stories become, **her language, so precise and beautiful, shines a light** so that you can go deeper into these worlds, where no one else has ever been. A wonderful debut."
—KEVIN WILSON, author of *The Family Fang*

"The force of *Night Beast* is seismic; I was startled to read a first book so **daringly original.** Ruth Joffre's dissident, imperiled characters are intricately drawn and deeply surprising. While working in the tradition of Djuna Barnes, Isak Dinesen, Ursula K. Le Guin, and Mary Gaitskill, Ruth Joffre manages to be sui generis, **a singular young writer reconfiguring the possibilities of fiction** at the dawn of—please gods—a dazzling career. There is nothing like her. And there never was."
—ALICE FULTON, author of *Barely Composed*

"Captivating . . . A cri de coeur for sympathy and understanding."
—PUBLISHERS WEEKLY

Night
Beast

Night Beast

and other stories

RUTH JOFFRE

Black Cat
New York

Versions of the stories collected here were originally published in the following publications: "Nitrate Nocturnes," in *Lightspeed Magazine*, April 2018; "Softening," in *SmokeLong Quarterly*, October 2016; "Go West, and Grow Up," in *Kenyon Review*, 34.4; "One of the Lies I Tell My Children (#5)" (from "Two Lies"), in *Juked*, April 2017; "General, Minister, Horse, Cannon," in *Mid-American Review*, 36.1; "The Ithaca Moment," in *Hayden's Ferry Review*, November 2013; "Safekeeping," in *DIAGRAM*, 17.1; "Night Beast," in *Master's Review*, March 2017.

FIRST EDITION

Published simultaneously in Canada
Printed in the United States of America

First Grove Atlantic paperback edition: May 2018

This book was designed by Norman Tuttle at Alpha Design & Composition

This book was set in 11.5pt Sabon by Alpha Design & Composition of Pittsfield, NH

Library of Congress Cataloging-in-Publication data available for this title.

ISBN 978-0-8021-2808-9
eISBN 978-0-8021-4627-4

Black Cat
an imprint of Grove Atlantic
154 West 14th Street
New York, NY 10011

Distributed by Publishers Group West

groveatlantic.com

18 19 20 21   10 9 8 7 6 5 4 3 2 1

for my mother

"I have been loved," she said, "by something strange, and it has forgotten me."

—Djuna Barnes, *Nightwood*

CONTENTS

Night Beast

Nitrate Nocturnes

Fiona's timer read: 40 33 04 21 53 08. Years, weeks, days, hours, minutes, seconds. Her first girlfriend had done the math one day in bed. "You'll be sixty-four when you meet your soul mate. I'll be twenty-two," the girl said with a gesture that revealed her frail, luminous wrist, which was lit from within, like a lightning bug. Fiona watched her own timer tick down through her girlfriend's hair, feeling as though she were trying to catch up to the world, as though she'd always be one step behind. One day, she would reach completion: 00 00 00 00 00 00. Her timer would ring out, as if she had just won a sweepstakes at a supermarket, and the numbers inside her wrist would flash repeatedly before fading quietly into her skin. But the timer could not tell her if she would be happy. Oftentimes, soul mates, having spent their entire lives waiting for completion, had to reconcile their fantasies of the future with a bleak and unsatisfying reality. Not all soul mates were immediately compatible, and not all soul mates fell in love. It could take years, decades—a whole lifetime, even—just to understand why. Why this person, of all people? It was all so unfair, Fiona whined, watching her girlfriend's timer. 06 29 05 14 50 07. 06. 05.

"You're just jealous," her girlfriend said with an ugly self-assurance.

Fiona should have broken up with the girl right then, but sixty-four years was a long time. Much too long to be alone, she knew. It was easier to stay—to wait—when there was someone to hold on to late at night, when the weight of years pressed down on her, making it hard to breathe. None of her lovers were meant for her, but she collected them all the same, cherishing what little time she had with them. And then she let them go, as if releasing paper lanterns at a wedding. She had watched with envy as her first girlfriend met her soul mate, learned his name, and proceeded to undo him—to uproot everything he thought he'd figured out about himself (his wants, his desires) and seed him with her favorite things, transforming him into the kind of person who wore boat shoes and drank good whiskey alone because he was ashamed. She'd always liked broken men. Fiona remembered this, just as she remembered the peculiarities of her first boyfriend's laugh, the imperial red jacket that attracted her to a one-night stand, and the strains of the jazz band in the background as one of her good friends confessed that she didn't know how to love her soul mate, because in her heart she'd been expecting someone different—quieter, kinder, cleaner. Fiona had loved them all with a kind of happiness that brings with it a relief from longing. For her own sake she'd learned not to isolate herself and to instead seek solace from others in a similar situation.

Her current boyfriend was Marcus, a dark, dispassionate Southerner with a resonant voice Fiona often described as oaky, like red wine. His timer read: 25 16 08 07 49 52. He'd be fifty-two, just ten days shy of fifty-three, when he found his soul mate, whom he imagined as a tall, willowy woman with gray hairs and pink reading glasses that matched the healthy color of her tongue. He was getting a PhD in sociology and intended to be a tenured professor by the age of forty, so that when he finally met his soul mate he would have his half of their life already prepared. Fiona met him at a graduate student mixer in the fall of her third year. She knew just from the calm way he fixed himself a drink without bothering to glance at her timer that he was like her: a long-gamer. He smiled when he finally noticed it. He led her outside, where they sat in the shadow of the barn where the mixer was being held. "It's curious," he said. "These short-timers act as if they're on the verge of unlocking all life's mysteries, like they're winning some sort of race toward maturity. But most of them can't fathom what it's like to wait. They're too impatient."

Fiona leaned back against the soft hay the owners had left out for show. "My mother used to tell me that a short timer isn't necessarily a blessing. My father was an alcoholic, and when she met him she was at some dive in Pittsburgh celebrating her twenty-first birthday. He said she just kept crying: 'He's so old. What am I supposed to do with him?' She wasn't prepared. None of them are." Marcus nodded, asking if it ended badly. When she told him that it had, he laid his hand quietly on hers and let her decide if she wanted the weight of it—the weight of his arms, his hips, their firm curves nestled between her legs as if he had all the time in the world. She'd invited him into her life in spite of his reputation for treating women like amusing diversions. Fiona had heard the story of a girl who went mad for him, having somehow managed to convince herself despite all the evidence to the contrary that their timers were wrong and Marcus was the one. He ended up having to get a restraining order. The experience left him wary of relationships, aware that women could break against him, like waves against a cliff. One night, he confessed all this to Fiona, then added that he liked her because she wouldn't break. She would outlast him, he said. When the years had worn him down as thin and soft as tissue, Fiona would still be standing, like a lighthouse on the shore.

When Fiona decided to move in with Marcus in the fall, her mother had misgivings. "It's a little early, don't you think? Most people don't settle in for the long wait until thirty."

Fiona was making dinner at the time, throwing lentils into a stockpot to simmer.

Her mother heard the clattering of pots. She sighed. "He can't even cook, can he?"

"He's just busy right now. He's preparing for his A exam."

"Don't you think you'd be happier with a woman? That's what you always wanted."

"I'm not unhappy with Marcus. He's safe. I need that right now."

Her mother paused. "Has it been bad?"

With a sigh, Fiona told her that most of the people in her program had already found their soul mates. One of them had asked his classmates to help him film the last hour of his wait. Six of them circled around, holding booms, pushing dollies, watching his face as he strutted through the halls of the performing arts building, smiling like an idiot. Fiona had criticized the project, called it self-indulgent and vacuous, something better suited for YouTube than a senior thesis, but when Fiona said this one of her classmates groaned, "God, why do you have to shit on everything? Just because it's sentimental doesn't mean it's stupid."

"That's ridiculous," Fiona's mother said. "You're the most sentimental person I know."

"Tell them that." She sighed, stirring the lentils. "I've started to hate going to class."

"It just sounds like they got a bad batch this year. Next year will be better."

"Next year five of them are going to meet their soul mates."

"Are they going to film those, too?"

Fiona laughed once but otherwise didn't respond.

"You know what you used to say to me, Fi? You said, 'Mama, I know who my soul mate is. I know her name.'" This started when she was a little girl and first took up watercolor. Her mother didn't understand her sudden fascination with art and music, because before that she'd never even been interested in finger painting. When asked why the sudden change, Fiona fixed her mother with a long, baleful look and said, 'This is how I meet her, Mama. This is the best way,' as if she'd considered all their possible futures together and determined that this one would be the best, the happiest. "That kind of conviction is rare, Fi. Don't forget it."

Fiona nodded and said goodbye, but the truth was that she didn't remember saying that. What prompted it? What had she known that her timer hadn't? It frightened Fiona to think that there was or could be more than one possible future. Was this, in fact, Fiona's best possible life?

Her timer read: 40 33 03 16 23 08. 07. 06. 05.

Fiona finished cooking the soup and invited Marcus over. Then, when he had come in her mouth and fallen asleep on the sofa, she reconsidered the numbers pulsing on her wrists. In them, Fiona could see her future laid out, like a series of milestones hidden inside a digital alarm clock: in one month, she and Marcus would sign a lease on a new apartment for the fall semester; in just three weeks, she would have midterms; in April, she would fly down to Mississippi with Marcus, where his family would either approve or disapprove of his choice in a waiting partner; and then nothing, absolutely nothing. Darkness stretched out before her like a sheet, obscuring everything, even her timer. How long would the darkness last, she wondered. Late at night, when the campus emptied, Fiona climbed down into one of the gorges, bringing only a video camera and a thermos of coffee. Earlier that semester, fences had been installed on all the bridges on campus to prevent students from jumping off. Fiona's latest project was to film these students from below, zooming in until their faces blurred together into a single, tremulous mass. Fiona understood their fear, the way it circled them like an owl gliding toward its prey. No matter how hard she tried, she couldn't shake the thought that she had taken a wrong turn, lost sight of what was most important in life. She was on the verge of ending things with Marcus when her timer began speeding up.

It started in class: a brief flash, immediately followed by a sound like a hiccup in her right wrist when her timer whirred into its new position: 40 23 06 19 47 08. One hour had been lopped off her original time, bringing her incrementally—and unexpectedly—nearer her completion date of 2047. Her friend Siobhan, sitting next to her, hurried to explain what happened to their curious classmates, and their teacher, a prim blond woman in her mid to late fifties, lifted Fiona's arm, scrutinizing it carefully. "I've heard of this happening," their teacher said, sounding disappointed, because Fiona's numbers had stopped whirring and they wouldn't be able to film it in real time. "I know there are researchers in Canada who've filmed a man's timer growing longer, but no one to my knowledge has managed to capture the reverse phenomenon—yet." Though it happened four more times during that class, none of them aimed a camera at her wrist, not because she would've objected but because they didn't honestly believe it would happen again. Each time her wrist hiccupped, Fiona jumped, and her classmates gazed at her in wonder, as if she'd prove interesting after all. She was invited to a party that night, to everyone's surprise. She didn't bring Marcus.

Her timer had shaved off forty-three hours by the time she arrived at the house. She could hear laughter swelling in the backyard. Siobhan was there with their classmates and a few people she had seen walking around between classes. Her cheeks were nearly frozen. She happily joined them in front of the fire pit, where she perched on a log and accepted a cup of mulled wine. Their host said, "Someone's excited," with a knowing smirk.

Fiona just blushed and pulled her sleeve farther down her wrist.

Curious, the host settled beside Fiona on the log. "I'm Roman. Ramona to my mother."

Fiona nodded through the steam of her mulled wine. "Have we met before?"

"No, but I believe you know Matt," she said, pointing across the fire pit to a schlubby guy with a frosted beard and a lumberjack's cap. "He's my guy. My rock."

Fiona looked Matt up and down. "He seems very sturdy."

Roman sputtered beer, laughing. "Matt said you were a bitch. In a good way, I promise."

This did not faze Fiona. She had heard it before. She turned to Siobhan, who walked over with a bag of marshmallows and the fixings for s'mores. "Just one," she said, pointing to Roman. "I know how you get."

Roman, who had already stuffed two marshmallows in her mouth, lifted her hands as if to say, "I'm innocent. Don't shoot."

Siobhan scowled. "Don't give me that face. I'm on to you. Go find me some sticks."

With an exaggerated pout, Roman trudged into the house in search of roasting forks.

Once alone, Siobhan whispered to Fiona, "Everyone's talking about your timer."

Fiona shrugged. "I'm more interested in whatever's going on between you and Roman."

Siobhan smirked but didn't deny it. Her mischievous gaze drifted to where Roman and Matt stood framed in the small window of the kitchen. Matt had taken off his lumberjack cap and matching jacket and appeared to be snickering at something Roman had said. His flask rose to his lips, but Roman took it away from him before he could drink. He didn't take offense at this or demand it back, only rolled up his sleeves and set about doing dishes while Roman returned with three roasting forks. Matt looked up briefly and waved to Fiona where she sat wondering if that was what happiness was made of: confidence, ease. Having refilled her cup of wine and located a half-full box of graham crackers, Roman plunked herself down in the grass and began loading a roasting fork with marshmallows. "How many you want?" she said, asking Fiona.

"All of them."

Roman laughed, holding ten over the fire. "I like your style."

Fiona crouched next to the fire, holding her graham crackers at the ready.

Siobhan laughed. "It's gonna be a minute, Fi."

"I know. I wish I'd brought my camera." Hovering above the flame, the pale underbellies of the marshmallows began slowly to caramelize, reminding Fiona of a burning filmstrip—how the celluloid bubbled, then burst, leaving browned pockets of color where images used to be. She had burned an entire movie once—shot it on a reel of over-exposed Super 8 film, then lit it on fire one frame at a time just to see it for herself—just because, she told them. She remembered seeing the image of her own hand glowing hot in the flames, the fingers and palm turning orange, losing shape. Roman deposited the roasted marshmallow on her graham cracker just as it began to ooze. "Thank you," she breathed. After one bite, her phone flashed. Marcus had texted. *You up?* It took some doing to write back without getting chocolate and marshmallow on her phone.

Her frustrated growl made Siobhan giggle. "Not in the mood tonight?"

"I'm just really into this s'more. It's my boyfriend now."

Siobhan tilted her head like a psychiatrist. "You seem to have a thing for dark chocolate."

Fiona was in the middle of a bite and could only mumble the words "shut up."

Roman leaned back, loading another set of marshmallows. "You seein' someone, Fiona?"

She nodded, waving her hand as if it meant nothing. "Marcus. He might come."

"He know about your timer?"

This question surprised Fiona, who had never considered the possibility that the single most essential thing about her—the length of her wait—could shrink inside her, become small and dark and secretive, like the inside of a camera, where images wait to be found. Her number seemed to change of its own volition, losing a minute here, an hour there, without asking her consent or giving her time to adjust to her new identity. When in the light of the fire her timer began to wail, spinning and stopping and then spinning again, her brain, fuzzed over from wine, struggled to understand just what was happening from one moment to the next and couldn't process the numbers: 00 18 05 23 14 06. Then: 42 05 06 14 38 02. And then: 00 26 06 09 14 23. It lingered on this last time long enough that people began to do the math.

"Twenty-six weeks. That would be . . . August."

"Summer? Orientation, maybe."

"You think it could be a prospective student?"

When her timer began to vacillate between August and March, it became clear: this was a prospective student (a graduate student, she hoped) who'd been admitted to several programs and was deciding between them, wondering which ones they would visit. Fiona's timer suggested they'd decided on her school, but then all of a sudden rolled itself back to the beginning, to: 40 23 04 13 47 06. Her friends leaned back. One of them said, "Oh," unwilling to voice what they were all thinking: that Fiona's soul mate had chosen not to come, and there was nothing Fiona could do about it. When she looked up, she saw Marcus's face materialize in the shadows, his broad mouth and distin-guished stubble lit from below by his phone; the mere sight of him there made her want to cry.

Marcus comforted her as best he could. He walked her home after the party and let her cry herself out, then he kissed her, his warm satin kisses proceeding his fingers as he told her to relax. He took his time, thinking this would soothe her, but when it was over and he was in the shower she went rummaging through a box of old clothes for a pair of leather cuffs that her father had made for her before he died. "Timers can be so cruel," her father had said, fastening the cuffs around her wrists to hide the numbers glowing under her skin; he had sobered up by then. Thirteen years of hard work on her mother's part had turned him into the man her timer had anticipated and demanded. United, they brought out the best possible ver-sions of each other; that was what made them soul mates. Patient and considerate, humbled by his alcoholism and his past, Fiona's father tried making amends with small acts of kindness like the cuffs; then, one day, at an ATM not far from their house, he was killed in broad daylight by a high school senior attempting his first robbery. "I needed the money," the teenager said in custody. "I'm supposed to meet my soul mate in a month and I need to support her."

Someone had carved their numbers into the wall of the library: 33 19 06 15 47 03. No one knew if the numbers belonged to a real human being or if they'd been auto-generated by the artist under the cover of night, but every-one understood the meaning of the title: I REFUSE. When people began adding their own numbers to this list, critics noted with some disdain that all of them belonged to long-gamers and that the piece smacked of a kind of juvenile self-pity in which only a disgruntled and unloved artist could indulge. But then short-timers began adding their numbers, as did professors and enders who had long since reached their completion date. Fiona was surprised both that the list had filled the library's western wall and that the administration allowed it to continue even after campus religious groups referred to the piece as an abomination. In their opinion, timers were a gift from God, and reject-ing that gift was a form of blasphemy.

Marcus asked if she was going to add her name to the wall. She hesitated. "Are you?"

"I just think it's silly," Marcus said, watching people scratch their numbers into the wall with keys and scissors. "You can't escape fate. Even if you do reject your timer, it's going to count down anyway. You're going to meet your soul mate. So why fight it?"

Fiona dipped her head. "Don't you find it exhausting? Living up to these expectations."

He shrugged, setting his coffee on the table. "I'm a patient man."

His remarkable self-assurance made Fiona uneasy, and she regretted having joined him in the library café. Exhausted by a nasty sinus infection she'd been fighting since mid-March, Fiona lifted her gaze, head wobbling as she glanced around the room. It seemed everywhere she looked harried students were working at a feverish pace, desperate to return to their nice warm beds. Her brain felt like a watercolor, its pale amorphous lobes ridding the world of its edges, and her thick, phlegmy cough rattled in her chest like the cogs of a broken-down machine.

"Fiona," Marcus said, reaching out to touch her hand. "You need to get some rest."

Fiona withdrew, pulling her sleeves down to hide her cuffs. "I just need to finish this."

Marcus sat back, disappointed. "You shouldn't be wearing those things."

"That's not your decision to make."

"Suit yourself."

Fiona blinked up at him, wondering when he stood. "Are you leaving?"

"I'm just getting another coffee. Do you want one?"

Fiona felt her mind nod irrespective of her head. As Marcus walked off, the asymmetrical patterns of his turtleneck unhinged, like the colorful pieces of a tangram she couldn't fit back into its box. He used to make sense to her, but ever since the night in front of the fire he felt different.

She had begun distancing herself from him, making room for her soul mate, in case she arrived early. Of late, she had taken to imagining that her soul mate had already arrived, that she could sense this woman all around: in her house, in her bed, lingering beside her as she got dressed and went outside to greet the world with a secret happiness, a kind of intricate joy that kept her from feeling alone. Once or twice, she told Marcus, she'd even caught herself thinking in terms of "the two of us," her and her soul mate, as if she were making decisions for the both of them.

When he returned, she was doodling in her notebook. "What's that?"

"A picture," she said, rotating the book so he could see: a woman's head, its rounded chin and high, elegant forehead framed by a ring of loose curls. Fiona imagined the curls were blond, but otherwise had no real insight into the woman's precise features. "I wish I could see her face." Where the nose and mouth would be, she had drawn a blank.

"Fiona. This is unhealthy. You have to keep living your life."

"What if she decided not to come because she doesn't want to see me?"

Marcus wiped his hand over his temple. "We've been over this. You can't know what her intentions are; you're just guessing that she's a prospective student. There's no proof."

16

Fiona shook her head. She did know. That night by the fire, one word had passed through her mind: "money," its sad truth ringing like wires that had suddenly been drawn taut in the back of her brain. That was the reason her soul mate originally decided not to come. Fiona's private liberal arts college was prohibitively expensive for most people, and if not for her father's life insurance payout Fiona wouldn't have been able to attend, even with a scholarship and stipend. Sometimes she wondered if her soul mate's timer had sped up, too, and if she'd known when she first decided not to come what that would mean. But Fiona couldn't really believe that, and she placated her gnawing fears with thoughts of the future: growing basil, mending dresses, walking hand in hand down streets painted with red leaves, their pale pink underbellies, thin as paper and just as lined.

Without realizing it, Fiona had begun to cry.

Marcus shut his book. "She's not going to like you like this."

"I know." She said this quietly, mournfully, turning so she would not have to see his face. Her gaze drifted toward a tiny swaddled freshman girl who floated in and out of the crowd gathering at the art installation. Had she seen this girl before? Fiona couldn't remember anymore. Faces had started blurring together, appearing once, sharply, then receding into a haze Fiona could no longer decipher or distinguish. Her only thoughts upon seeing someone new were "that's not her" and "don't worry." It had been a long time since she last hung out with friends or with anyone besides Marcus. Siobhan had taken her to coffee two weeks before, and Roman had, with Matt's blessing, invited her to dinner. But Fiona had declined. She knew it would only make them uncomfortable to see her like this. She did not want their pity.

When she turned back around, Marcus had already left.

That night, awakened by her coughing, Fiona pulled on her boots and mittens and trudged through the deserted campus, photographing the snow, which rose and fell like sand dunes on the Arts Quad. Halfway to the library, Fiona stumbled across a peculiar set of tracks in the blanket of fresh snow: big, plodding boot prints (almost certainly male) accompanied by a deep gouge made with a heavy object of some kind—perhaps a machine. Hidden behind a tree, Fiona screwed on a telephoto lens and pointed it at the library's western wall, where a man stood on a tall ladder. His hands and face were obscured from this angle, but judging by height alone Fiona guessed this was the unknown artist behind I REFUSE. Getting closer, she realized he had deepened the numbers scratched into the stone earlier and was adding new ones above them:

21 37 06 09 45 02

05 09 01 42 53 28

56 37 04 03 29 08

18

Half an hour later, the artist descended the ladder and began slowly dragging it back to his hiding place inside the fine arts building. His tracks would be filled by morning, Fiona knew, so nobody would be able to follow them or uncover his identity. She would keep his secret. She didn't tell anyone that she added her numbers to the wall. Her video camera, stationed some thirty feet to the right, recorded her untying her leather cuffs, considering her timer, and then covering it again before scratching her numbers into the wall from memory: 40 19 03 07 49 18. Ever since the fire, she had been counting down her original timer in her head, comparing what it would've read had it never changed to what it read now. This was her secret: that the morning after she put on the cuffs her timer began whirring indecisively, resetting itself every night for a month before finally settling on a time: 00 22 05 03 16 35.

Her soul mate would be arriving in the fall.

Fiona started preparing in August, when she moved into the new one-bedroom apartment she'd originally intended to live in with Marcus during the long wait. He'd taken his name off their lease at her request and later helped her move her heavy furniture into the apartment, lifting, hauling, and reassembling as if he actually intended to be her friend. In truth, his interest in her had long since waned and become primarily physical, and now whenever he came over there was a faint air of bemusement about him, as if he couldn't understand why she insisted on playing house alone. He studied her table lamps, her stoneware plates, the new down comforter she made him turn down before getting into bed, wondering if this was what she liked or what she believed she should like for her soul mate. It was all so strange to him. "I feel like I'm eating another man's food," he told her once over dinner, not because it upset him but because he'd never been in such a position before and found it rather intriguing. From a sociological perspective, he assured her.

Fiona's mother worried she was getting a little ahead of herself.

"Timers aren't supposed to do that, Fi. What did your doctor say?"

"What they all say: 'Blah blah blah, there's still a lot we don't know about timers, blah.'"

"Did he run any tests?"

"Waiting for the results. But I doubt they'll find anything if they don't know what they're supposed to be looking for." Her doctor had been wholly unwilling to think there was anything at work other than Fiona's romanticized ideals, but Fiona had her own theory about what was going on. Her research revealed rare cases in which timers had gone dark, their numbers appearing to be erased, only to turn back on, weeks or months later, for reasons that weren't entirely clear. The timers, it seemed, weren't perfect and didn't account for accidents and random acts of violence. They couldn't predict if a person would be satisfied with their soul mate or if that would have to wait for the next life—or the next. Perhaps dissatisfaction had led her soul mate to make a life-altering decision that changed the course of their future; then again, maybe it was fear.

Weeks passed, and Fiona couldn't get the thought out of her head. "What if she's running from something?"

Siobhan pushed her glasses back. "Who?"

Fiona blinked. "Oh, I didn't realize I said that out loud."

"Jesus Christ, Fiona."

Fiona shrugged defensively. "I'm allowed to worry, given the circumstances."

Siobhan sighed, running a hand over her face. "Can we please just finish this project?"

"Right. Of course." A second later, Fiona asked, "You going to the party tonight?"

Siobhan dropped her head into her book, pounding it in frustration.

"I'll take that as a yes."

While getting dressed that night, Fiona decided to unlace her leather cuffs. Her timer read: 00 03 01 16 38 02—three weeks, one day, sixteen hours, thirty-eight minutes, and two seconds to completion. It amazed her how quickly the timer was counting down now that the first two digits had reached zero. Fiona had waited twenty-four years for this sight; now whenever she saw it she flushed with pride, as if it were a reward for her hard work and determination. Siobhan would die if she knew.

Fiona arrived late to the party. "Daydreaming again?" Siobhan asked.

Fiona laughed but didn't deny it. "What kind of cake did you get?"

"Double-double chocolate."

Fiona joined Siobhan at the tail end of the bar, where she was busily counting out candles for Roman and Matt, whose birthdays were just forty-five hours apart. Both of them were turning twenty-eight. "Are all these people here for the party?" Fiona craned her neck over the crowd.

Siobhan glanced over her shoulder. "I think so. You should go say hi to Roman."

Fiona pushed off the bar, through the gaps between bodies. Peanut shells cracked underneath her boots. Classmates milled about, drinking well liquors and two-dollar cans of PBR. One of the local pool hustlers missed a shot Fiona had seen him make fifty times. Way in the back of the bar, Fiona found her friends: the birthday boy and girl were nestled in a booth, arms thrown around each other as they ate fries and mean mugged for the camera.

"Fiona!" Roman said, french fries still dangling from her lips.

Fiona lifted her eyebrows in surprise. "You changed your hair."

A blue shock of hair rose in a ponytail from the center of her otherwise shaved head.

"You like it? Matt did it himself."

Matt nodded drunkenly. Five empty beer cans sat in front of him.

After Fiona pulled up a chair, Roman leaned over and whispered conspiratorially, "Fiona. I need to talk to you about Siobhan. I can't seem to get through to her. Can you hook me up?"

Fiona glanced at Matt, then back at Roman. "I thought you two . . ."

"What— Matt? No. He's like my little brother. I've known him since I was two."

Fiona understood now. Matt and Roman were platonic soul mates, life partners who found romantic fulfillment in others. This sort of arrangement was not uncommon, particularly among those of different sexual orientations or religious faiths, but Fiona herself had never met a couple like this before; she found it refreshing. "I can talk to Siobhan, but we all know she's into you."

Roman nodded glumly. "Maybe. But that's not the same thing as wanting to be with me."

"It doesn't have to be." Fiona shrugged. "Just wait and see what happens."

Matt grinned, lifting his beer in toast. "To putting yourself out there!" Only then did Matt realize Fiona didn't have a drink. "Can I get you something? An old-fashioned?"

His face when she said no made her laugh and suggest a game of pool to cheer him up.

He rubbed his hands together gleefully. "Prepare to lose."

Fiona snickered, allowing the giddiness of the night to seep into her. She was terrible, just incapable of playing pool with grace or skill, but she did like listening to the balls clack around on the felt, their hard, shiny resin gleaming in the light of the low-hanging lamps. In between turns, she watched Matt's stripes roll and spin as he attempted shots he wasn't capable of yet, shots that sent billiard balls flying into the crowd, where Matt's party guests dodged them with increasing skill. Fiona followed these runaway balls under stools and jukeboxes, wondering when she did if anyone would see the numbers on her timer or if they were more concerned with the eight ball upending itself at their feet. During one of these retrieval missions, someone from a class she'd taken asked if he knew her. When she shook her head, she noticed that her timer had grown soft and that the numbers in each column had gotten stuck, trapped somehow between two and three, six and seven, one and zero. Puzzled, she looked up at the stranger, who shook his head, knowing he wasn't the one. Fiona glanced around, seeking new faces, ones she thought she could trust. And then, when she turned, her timer blared its end: 00 00 00 00 00 00.

Here she was: gray eyed, smartly dressed, with painted nails that glinted like the surface of the ocean at night. Fiona's soul mate stared at her in a state of wonder and disbelief. Her lips parted, and Fiona felt a sudden wash of affection. She felt her life aligning inside her, like the gears of a puzzle box turning, clicking into place in preparation for the moment it would be solved. With equal parts hope and sadness, Fiona's soul mate pulled back her sleeve, revealing her wrist. Her timer hadn't stopped.

"Oh," Fiona said, grabbing her wrist like a prisoner released from handcuffs. Her face felt totally numb, and she was shivering inside her winter coat. Her soul mate touched her arm gently, but she couldn't feel it through the puffy sleeve. For some reason, Fiona said, "I'm sorry."

"It's not your fault. My timer must be wrong," the woman said, even as a man grabbed her elbow with a familiarity that said she was his for now. Marianne, he called her, tugging on her arm with just enough force to make her take a step toward him. "Just give me a minute," she said.

Feeling light-headed, Fiona staggered back, as if about to faint. "I have to go."

"No," Marianne started to say, but, distraught, Fiona turned around and headed straight to the door, remembering only at the last second to drop her billiard ball into the palm of a bemused but not unreceptive stranger who wished her a good night. Outside, the cold midnight air soothed her, and after several deep breaths she was able to remember which way to walk to get home. For a moment she considered dipping into the bar's alley, resting her head against its cool stone walls as she thought of the neon signs inside, of the gratifying curves of the ancient jukebox, and of the thin hearts carved into the wooden tables and booths. But there were people sitting on the steps of the bar, and she didn't want any of them to see her like this. She'd come too early, Fiona realized. She'd made a mistake. Marianne's timer didn't know her yet.

Her timer was still visible. Its numbers had turned black and had stopped glowing, but the individual digits had not faded into her skin, lingering there months after completion. Their presence mocked her, making her think of branded cattle or of whirlwind lovers tattooing their bodies with the initials of their beloved: MQ, Marianne Quennell, daughter of Mia Noémie and Edouard Jérôme Quennell, two linguistics professors at the University of Victoria in British Columbia, where Marianne lived until she decided to attend graduate school in the United States. Perhaps this explained the indecisiveness of her timer. It must've been a difficult decision leaving home, particularly when home was so very beautiful. Fiona had seen photographs online: of the ferries Marianne rode across Puget Sound, of the books she read and the misty beaches where she lounged, watching pods of orcas drift past.

What had brought her to this cold, snowy campus, where the prettiest thing was the sound of a waterfall roaring beneath your feet?

Apparently, Marianne had a long-term boyfriend. Charles Tremblay. The man who held her arm at the bar that night. "I guess she tried to break up with him before she moved here," Siobhan said, having heard the story from a friend of a friend. "But he wouldn't let her go. He called and texted until finally he wore her down and she agreed to take him back. I give it another month, tops."

Fiona blinked a few times, just trying to absorb the information, but she couldn't seem to fit it inside her head. Siobhan had dropped in on her at a bad time, while she was looking at a series of homemade videos shot by people who had rejected their timers: people who attempted to cut out, burn off, or otherwise remove the numbers from under their skin. Fiona was barely able to gather herself and now sat on the far end of the couch, hugging a pillow to her chest.

"She wants to see you."

Fiona shook her head. The mere thought of it was unbearable.

"You can't stay cooped up in here. It isn't healthy. You have to go out. Shoot a movie."

"I'm not sure I want to be a director anymore," Fiona said, pulling at a loose thread.

"That's nonsense and you know it."

"I just feel like I've spent my whole life making myself into this thing. And for what?"

Siobhan considered her for a moment. "You couldn't have known this would happen, Fi."

Thinking back on it, though, part of her had known. On her fifth birthday, her mother had recorded her having a conversation with her great aunt. Fiona was caught saying of her soul mate, "She's very pretty. She has curly blonde hair and speaks with a French accent." When asked how she knew all this, young Fiona grinned knowingly and said, "She told me." It seemed so innocent at the time, just another childish fantasy played out in the living room while her mother spoke on the phone.

Now, years later, thinking back on the conversation gave Fiona a sinking feeling deep in her stomach. She feared she'd been lying to herself, pretending she was prepared for the long wait, when in fact she was just drowning. In her lowest moments, Fiona texted Marcus and asked him to come over—but he was rougher than she remembered, his thrusts sharp and selfish and his hands bruising, as if using her to work through some dark and buried anger. It frightened her to think what she'd become to him. How ridiculous she looked now.

It had been three months. Fiona rarely left the apartment except for class.

Occasionally, she rallied, braving the cold for a trip to the library or a night at the cinema. Fiona felt safe there, in the silence of the theater, where the heated stairs and the scent of buttered popcorn transported her to another world. This was her sole comfort in the dark, early days of the year. More often than not, the sun set shortly before Fiona crawled out of bed, making it feel like no time had passed at all. Life was just one long night stretching into eternity. December became January. Monday became Tuesday. Fiona's mother grew worried. "What happened to that doctor you were talking to? What was his name?"

"He was a researcher, Mom. He wasn't interested in me. Just my timer."

"Well, did he at least figure out what was wrong?"

"Nothing's wrong. She just isn't the one. Or I'm not her one."

In the silence, Fiona imagined the angry line of her mother's frown.

"Anyway, I'm fine. I'm going to a party tonight. An Elegant Winter Party."

"Please tell me it's not another one of those ridiculous mixers they hold in a barn."

"For your information, it's a fund-raiser for the cinema, and I'm excited about going."

That year's theme was the Roaring Twenties. Attendees were encouraged to wear period costumes and buy drinks at the bar. On the walk over, Fiona saw more than a few tipsy donors in flapper dresses and cloche hats traipsing through the snow. Inside, ushers in tuxedo-mimicking T-shirts checked coats and directed guests toward the hors d'oeuvres table. Fiona lingered for some time over the miniature quiches, pleased by the compliments she received on her cocktail dress: a satiny black sheath with gauzy sleeves and a dramatic white sash that flowed down from her bust to her stockinged feet. In it, she felt like someone other than herself—the product of a bygone era whose passing had left her radiant and sophisticated but not at all prepared to see Marianne.

"Hello. It's Fiona, yes?"

Fiona shivered with fear and hope. "I wasn't expecting to see you here."

"Yes, well, I thought you might come tonight, and I love the cinema." Marianne shrugged prettily, with a motion that caused the silver tassels of her dress to shimmer around her throat. As she smiled, the halide lamps in the ceiling warmed up, glowing a soft pink. Marianne pointed up. "We had these in Vancouver, too, but ours were yellow." Her eyes fell to Fiona's. "It's softer, no?"

Fiona did her best not to blush. "I think they only turn them on for special occasions."

Marianne hummed quietly, pleased to have Fiona's attention. "Have you seen this film?"

Fiona shook her head. Marianne's finger was pointing at the screen, conjuring the pictures Fiona knew from this fund-raiser's invitations: a woman smiling in her lover's arms, a man gazing up at the newly risen moon, two lovers clinging to each other on a riverbank—the man reclining, the woman resting her hand over his heart. Fiona remembered working at a theater much like this one in high school and standing onstage, allowing the bright light of the 35mm projector to shine over her head and superimpose images of cows, aliens, and sunrises on her face. In this state, she watched a coworker at the back of the theater signal with his hands: adjust the curtains, raise the volume, pull the focus, perfect. She told Marianne that every time she walked on that stage it was like stepping through a portal into a world of light and magic. Before love, before time, there was only this: endless, soundless ecstasy.

Marianne's eyes sparkled. "Maybe one day I will get to see this preshow, as you call it."

Fiona smiled sadly. "You can't. Everyone's switching to digital now."

"Pity." Marianne glanced around, then touched Fiona's arm lightly. "Shall we sit?"

"You don't have to do this," Fiona said, withdrawing. "You don't have to be nice to me."

"I want to." Marianne pressed a hand to Fiona's cheek, giving her a kind, confident smile. When Fiona protested that Marianne wasn't meant for her (that she had someone else, a soul mate waiting for her on the other end of her timer), Marianne hushed her with a soft clicking noise and assured her there could be any number of reasons their timers hadn't synced up. "Please, let's just sit down." She'd picked out two seats for them near the back of the theater, on the aisle to the left of the stage, where the pianist would walk when the lights began to dim. Fiona noticed as she settled in that the small track lights bordering the aisle were orange and that they shone faintly on Marianne's sparkly hemline. While she sat, her eyes fixed on Marianne's timer, the famed pianist accompanying the film delivered a lecture on its history. Evidently, its original negative had been destroyed in a big fire in Little Ferry, New Jersey, when a vault of nitrate films suddenly went up in flames. While she listened, Fiona couldn't help thinking that she should've known this already, should've known that desire was a spectacle and that she would spend all her time with Marianne contorting herself into the woman she thought her soul mate wanted. She accepted this future like she accepted the premise of a film with no color and no audio. In the gaps between chords, Fiona heard nothing, only the soft, sure sound of Marianne breathing in the dark.

SOFTENING

I used to tell people that my first kiss was on a December night, under a pine tree, when a boy I sort of liked kissed me after a dance recital; but actually my first kiss was older and with a woman. In this memory, I'm twelve, and I wake up one day to find the condo hushed, as if afraid to breathe too deep and set the hinges to sighing. I open my window to let the air lap at my legs. It rained overnight. I can smell it. I head to the bus early to enjoy it, the silence of the wet-blackened street and the fog clinging to the tires of the school bus. I feel as soft as a lick of shed fur, standing there, then watching houses roll past. By the end of second period the moisture in the air has lulled me to sleep.

It is the teacher who wakes me. Ms. Laura, I call her. She has one hand curved to my skull, her palm a constant heat seeping into my ears. She says, "Stay, eat lunch with me," then feeds me half a banana, hazelnuts, and a kind of candy—some strange, powdered things softening to the likeness of caramel and cream. She asks why I'm tired, why I'm hungry, and if I've eaten breakfast. I haven't. There were ants in my cereal I remember. I had to throw it out, box and all. Then, when some of the ants lingered in the bowl, I had to hold it up to the faucet and watch as the water rose slowly, slowly to drown them.

I don't remember if I tell her this or anything. I am aware that the lights are off, the door open, the halls bright, but quiet, while all the other students are at lunch. The static lines of a tape rewinding fall between us, that section of the in-class movie revealing a boy's throat opening and closing underwater. Maybe it's a trick of the light when a dog is resurrected on-screen and then again when Ms. Laura promises she will never hurt me, paint me in her chameleon colors with no more than the swift sure strokes of her voice. It's mournful work, this deciphering of hues, with the sun a dapple on the soft kid of Ms. Laura's boots and my right eye pressed to her shoulder until color begins unraveling on the lid: violet dots, a faint blue, millions of tiny stars winking, and a strange gold specter passing through. This is broken by the fingers smeared on my cheeks and the mouth tending to mine as to a bruise. Then this is broken by a knock next door, and Ms. Laura pulls back and never tries to comfort me again, perhaps because I have never learned how to ask for help or to realize that I need help when I need it. I let myself go hungry for entire weeks before speaking to Ms. Laura again, and then it's just to say that I finished my test. Very good, she says. Thank you.

Go West,
and Grow Up

We had been living in the car for the better part of a year when my mother left my father. I never thought she would have the strength. I had resigned myself to the life—the times my father fed me whiskey to keep me warm—until one night she decided enough was enough and pulled my father out of the backseat. My mother was not a strong woman, physically speaking, but he was too far gone to put up a fight. From the curb, she reached into the car, offering a hand to me. I took it a moment later, feeling the grease of my father's hair on her skin, then on mine. She worried that he would regain his motor skills, clamber back in the car, so she locked us in. When I leaned against her seat, she said, "Stay back. It's safe," and tried to start the engine several times. "My brother has a house in Oregon." The problem was: we were in Ohio.

* * *

Our objectives, on any given day, were simple: find food, get gas, stay warm. These often took so long that we didn't spend much time actually driving and instead hopped from town to town, earning pity. Sometimes it was by accident, just when we were waking up. Once, I was startled by the child outside my door—jumping, catching, releasing his balloon again—then by his mother, who upon seeing us offered some homemade cookies from a platter she had promised to a birthday party. Another time, a woman handed us her lottery ticket, a loser. I remember the first time best: the morning after we left my father in a gutter, waking to a knock on the window.

The night before, we had only enough gas to go a few miles, and my mother did not want to risk stranding us on a highway, so we only went as far as the nearest town. It was freezing. We huddled in the backseat with blankets piled on us (pulled over our heads, under our feet), creating a heat pocket. I listened to my mother breathe, the way the air went thick when she began to cry. I did not know how to quiet her, so I started crying, too. And we slept just like that, eyes gummy, bodies twisted to fit inside the shambles of our lives, until there was a second knock demanding to be acknowledged.

My mother sat up, smacking her tongue to dispel the fetid air that collects when you go to sleep on an empty stomach. I slid to the floor, where dirt stuck to my shins.

My mother rolled the window down and said hello with the exhausted, polite air of somebody who had been kicked out of a parking lot before.

"You need to get going."

"We need gas," my mother said, to which the man responded by looking out at the pumps and saying, slowly, "Well, this is a gas station."

My mother rubbed under her eye at the black smear of something, the stippling of our lives on the road and the faded contour of a bruise. She said, "Well, I have about fifty cents under this seat."

The man's eyes fell on me. He gripped the car, fingers on the inch of window that would not roll down anymore, hips jutting such that if I stretched my neck, I could see the back of his. I scratched aimlessly at my heel. He nodded at me and said, "When was the last time you ate?"

"The day before yesterday," I said, proud of the find and sorry at the same time that I had not made it last.

The man stuffed his hands in his jacket and peered hard at my mother. He said, "If I give you some money, will you buy food with it?" My mother nodded. The man motioned her toward him, saying, "Let me smell your breath." This was an embarrassment my mother never expected, but she had no reason not to do it. To his credit, he did not flinch at the smell. Luckily, he did not ask to smell my breath, too, because while my mother slept, I drank my father's old whiskey.

The man stood up so that I could no longer see his face, just a cutout of his torso through the window frame. His hands were fidgeting in his pockets; I could see that. I could hear his shoe against the asphalt, grinding against gravel, and I heard him cough, as my mother was petting my hair and moving to kiss its off-center part. She said, "Don't worry," and he bent again to say he would be back in a minute.

When he came back, my mother was standing, shaking out our blanket. I was kneeling on the floor of the car, taking the opportunity to brush out the crumbs, hairs, and accumulated filth of living in a tight space. Most of what I found belonged to my father: chipped cuff link, an empty pack of cigarettes, black sock, toenail clippings. These things I gathered in a pile by the door to be thrown away later.

The man returned carrying a plastic bag, which he handed to my mother. She closed it in one hand while attempting to gather a blanket with the other. She said, "Thank you." My mother was a gracious woman, but even she had her limits. He did not begrudge her these. He watched her buckle me in—a thing she never did again—then surround me with blankets. She did not hand me the bag; she did not have to.

He watched her thank him, again. That was what he was waiting for, I guess, because he said, "Pull up to one of the pumps."

He ambled over to the pumps, casting glances back to the convenience store. I did not see anyone through the glass, but perhaps he had told his manager what happened. Or perhaps he had not, and that was why he walked like a man whose every step would be accounted for later.

When he finished pumping, he knocked on the window. My mother cranked it down, just long enough for him to get his hands and his face in the crack. He said, "That should be half, maybe two-thirds of the tank." He looked around the car again with an expression I read and still read as gratitude: for his job, for being secure enough in his own lower-middle-class way to help someone who was worse off. On any other day, I might have hated him, but it was morning, and there were no other men in my life. My father would have been indignant, I think. He would have cussed upon being woken and not stopped until well after we drove off with not enough gas to go anywhere.

My mother, on the other hand, nodded, averting her eyes. She sighed. She could say thank you only so many times, so the man said, "Good luck," and left.

We started driving immediately. My mother did not look back, did not say anything, but I saw her tap the gas gauge to be sure it was accurate. I unbuckled myself, leaned against the back of the driver's seat, eyes cast around the corner of the headrest. I said, "I'm sorry," though I think I meant to say that it was nobody's fault, not even the gas station attendant's.

After an hour of driving, my mother finally pulled over and told me to climb up front. We spread the food out on the front seat: bottles of soda, a box of crackers, moon pies, packs of gum, one ice cream sandwich that had barely started to melt because we did not waste gas on heat, and other things, too: chips and gas station fare, including a burrito he hadn't taken the time to heat.

I said, "How much should we save for later?"

"Nothing," my mother said, opening a bottle of soda for me. "It's all expired."

We developed a routine to keep clean. My mother would send me into a gas station to get the bathroom key. We would strip down in the bathroom and string our clothes up so they would not touch the grimy floor. My mother would clean me from the top down—my head in the sink, to wash my hair with hand soap, my arms up and legs spread while carefully wet brown paper towels wiped the dirt away. We had learned that it was better to look poor or out of fashion than homeless and that if we were clean we could walk around all sorts of places like real people again, with a home and a dog to go back to later. We snuck into movie theaters simply by striding with purpose. I pickpocketed without ever being suspected. My mother stole shoes from department stores. We rarely got caught.

One night, in Nebraska, my mother informed me, "I have a plan." We were in a bathroom then, my mother plucking her eyebrows. I had done recon on the gas station's convenience store, its lone manager, who was not overweight exactly but seemed to hold himself as if he were used to being young and fit and did not appreciate the bulk tacked on to his body. I went in first, hood thrown up so the manager would not see my wet hair when I handed him the bathroom key. Then I walked around deliberately, picking things up, putting them down. I tried to look suspicious for the man so he would not bother with my mother, a pretty woman with her hair up in a tight bun—a decent customer, whereas I was a punk stealing a candy bar.

The man behind the counter did not fall for our trick. He lumbered over to me. Until then, I had not realized that he was so tall or that his arms were so muscled; these were things I keenly knew in the moment he gripped me. I tugged, just once, testing his strength. Then I fell quiet, like a wire.

He said, "Empty your pockets."

"I didn't steal," I said, my whole body aiming for the safety of the floor while he held my arm up and out at the elbow. My palm was upturned, my fingers curled tightly, so they wouldn't brush his chest; my nails were digging into my skin.

"Well," he said. "Then you should have no problem turning out your pockets."

I did this without fussing and with only one hand, reaching across and behind me, turning out every pocket, their fabrics dingy white, hanging like tongues. I felt the man's grip tighten. He was even more suspicious now that he saw I had absolutely nothing, not a single possession. He tugged my arm, pulling me so that I had to fight not to tumble into him. He seemed to like this effort. He said, "Come with me," but my mother did not allow this.

She spoke sharply and without compromise. "What's the problem here?"

The man wiggled me like a doll. "Is this your daughter?"

"Yes," my mother said, with some reluctance.

The man nodded. "What's in that purse?"

My mother stiffened and did not say a word. The man released me. "Follow me," he said, then led my mother into the back room. I was alone in the store, so I stuffed my pockets with Pop-Tarts and the small, expensive stuff I could find. I went behind the cash register, stared hard at its buttons. I picked pockets for a living and had broken a few locks, but I had never robbed a store like that. I did not know if I could: the register seemed secure, if untended. I pressed a button, but no luck. There was a lockbox under the counter. With the metal nail file I had hidden in the band of my underwear, the long sharp kind, I jimmied the lock. In the box, I found one hundred singles in a tight blue money wrap. These I tucked into my underwear.

I was standing in front of the door, holding the pointed end of the file where I figured the man's face would appear, when he came out again. He edged away from me, and

I followed. The point was sharp enough, his face soft enough. I could probably take out his eye, shove the end up his nostril, give him a lobotomy. I could still feel his hand on my arm, feel my mother shaking even as she passed me by for the hot food stand. I would have inflicted this violence upon him if she had asked me to. My mother handed me a hotdog instead.

We drove just far enough to be out of sight of the gas station before we pulled over on the frozen plain. My mother got out, peeling off her jacket. She stuck two fingers down her throat to make herself vomit.

I had in my pocket a small bottle of Listerine. I opened it and swilled the alcohol burn. In the grass, my mother was trying to wipe her face clean. I spat by the tires and then offered my mother the bottle. "Will this help?"

I picked up my mother's jacket, just high enough so that only the sleeves were left on the ground. My mother gargled several times before I said, "I stole something else." I reached for the money in my underwear, and my mother's gaze followed my hand quietly. If she was excited by the crisp bills or angry at me for stealing without her permission, she did not have strength enough to express it. She held out her hand. I gave her the money. We drove to the next town, where we filled our gas tank to the brim and bought things we felt we deserved: a small bottle of shampoo, a pack of plain T-shirts for each of us, and burgers at a fast-food place.

My mother ate slowly. I, on the other hand, was ravenous, so when I was finished I asked if I could also eat my mother's fries. She was not looking at me when she nodded. She was staring out the window, as if worried someone would come for me, claim the money we had spent, label me a thief and her a bad mother. It was a fear she thankfully did not allow herself long, and if people did think as much, they at least had the good sense not to shame themselves by saying it to our faces. My mother never told me exactly what happened—but I could see it in the way she shied away from the men on the road, the men who sometimes looked like they wanted to help us and sometimes looked like it was the furthest thing from their minds. If I had said anything that night, my mother would've cracked under her silence, so I said nothing and sharpened under mine.

We had stopped for the night near Fort Collins. We were still sleeping, the blankets wrapped so thick around us that we were not visible to most passersby, when the car began to rock. We woke to the sounds of banging, a handful of college-aged students striking the windows, yelling, "Wakey wakey," and laughing. I sat up and watched them circle the car, as if in a ritual, whistling now that my mother was climbing into the front seat. One of the boys stood in front of the car and started to mouth words at my mother, another opened his mouth and licked the window nearest to me—this was enough, I thought. I struck the inside of the window, and maybe it was the accumulated venom of years in my veins, or maybe it was a weakness the car had developed, but I struck the glass, and it cracked. The boy jumped back, and all fell silent around us. I glowered at the corner long after they had turned it, long enough that my mother had brushed her hair and gotten out of the car to inspect the damage. I got out and stood next to her.

Down the street, somebody was moving out. My mother went up to a woman loading box after box into a U-Haul to ask for tape. The woman walked over with my mother, chatting kindly—or at least not unkindly—while she kept tabs on her roll of packing tape, which my mother handed to me, saying, "You fix it." I made an X on the window, the way I had seen people do in the movies when they prepared for a tornado. To cut the tape, I used the blade from a broken pair of scissors, which I had kept in case of an emergency.

The woman said, "That car's seen some damage."

The tape would keep some of the cold from seeping through the crack I thought. Our car was not well insulated as it stood, so it would be no worse. But now it was marked: the window was a sign, something that could be seen on the highway clearer than chipped paint, easier than the debris in the backseat or the possessions packed in our trunk. Now it would be obvious that the tires needed air, that the antenna had snapped, that we would not pass inspection when this woman's gaze passed over the hole in my jeans and the sorry state of the upholstery.

The woman said, though we had not responded to her last remark, "Where you headed?"

I got out of the car to return the tape. My mother shut the door softly behind me, then said, "Oregon." It was something she had never told anyone but me. I tried to read her face then, but she had gone vacant somewhere in the Midwest and never really came back.

"Oregon? Good luck."

My mother nodded, her eyes on the sky. I could see her chest rise and fall, see her shiver, and I knew that if the woman did not leave soon, my mother would begin to cry and not be able to stop.

I stared at the woman. I had not made eye contact until then, so this got her attention. She said, "Do you need any help?"

I nodded toward the U-Haul. "It looks like you need help."

The woman turned to regard her possessions. She breathed on her hand, warmed her face. She said, "How about this: you two help me pack and load, and I pay you for your time?"

I agreed. Once my mother started moving, spurred by the prospect of some money and an honest day's work, she agreed, too. Her cheeks flushed with the effort expended in the hauling of books and lamps, all the luxuries we once took for granted.

When we were done loading everything the woman owned, she offered to buy us lunch. I had become wary of food—knowing how infrequently it could come—but my mother agreed. She seemed grateful for company and for this woman who on the cusp of her own change took our poverty in stride: it was not a handout, and she did not make herself out to be the kind who gave out of the goodness of her heart.

We walked to a diner a few blocks away. I heard a dog whine, so I ambled away from the adults. My mother snapped at me. I said, "I hear a dog," and because in addition to everything my dog died last year, my mother said she would order for me.

The dog stood when he saw me. He had been chained to a pipe for what looked like hours. I figured he was owned by one of the people who worked in the diner, judging by the way the dog's knees knocked and the way he knew to stand when he heard footsteps rounding the corner. I was not offering him anything; I did not have food, so the dog did not take kindly to me. He began to bark, his massive shanks and jowls swaying. He was bigger than I expected. I approached carefully, one hand out. Then when I got close enough, I whacked the dog hard on the nose, hard enough that he hung his head and began to cry. I rubbed his head where he was subdued by pain, scratched his ears, patted his side. I had the soft touch, when I wanted it, and in a minute he was mine, inching forward on his paws so he could lay his head on my knee.

The dog's ears rose when he heard footsteps around the corner. I looked up to see a man in an apron. He had tattoos on his hands, a gauge in one ear—remnants, I thought, from a misguided youth. He had a look on his face like he had been forced to take any job he could find. He was scratching the dog's ears vigorously—too roughly, I thought—when he said to me, "So you like my dog, little girl?"

"Yes," I said, though I did not like being called little or a girl.

The man said, "Maybe you could come around my place and play with him sometime." A tattooed hand reached out to touch my hair, but I jerked back, stood, said no. He slapped his hand on his knee and rose. He was a foot taller than me. He said, "It's just as well. I don't want trash in my house."

I punched him in the gut on instinct, without stopping to think, but his outcast life in Fort Collins, Colorado, had made him hard, too, and after taking a deep breath he laughed off my fist and grabbed me by the shoulders. He threw me against the wall, and my lungs jumped in fright. I could hear the dog growling; I could feel the hand almost tenderly cupping my throat. His thumb stroked my jawline. He kissed my nose, and when I winced at that he kissed me with his dry lips, his body bending over mine.

I was standing on my tiptoes. His other hand was inside my coat, sliding along the line between my jeans and the unraveling hem of my shirt. I bent one leg up, in, clamping my legs shut. He said, "Don't be coy. You must be earning a living somehow."

For a moment, I was not sure what he meant, perhaps because I was still young enough to have never been kissed, but, after a second, as the tattooed man began to fumble with my zipper, I realized that I had been spared the worst of it, that my mother had shielded my last shred of innocence for as long as she could. For the first time in months, I was keenly aware of how helpless I was, how I had dropped weight and muscle mass to the point where the force of kneeing the man in the groin fazed him for only a moment. That time was all I needed to break free from the hand he forgot to close around my throat. I hit him on the shoulder, and he pushed me as he staggered backward. When I hit the wall, the dog attacked.

The dog bit his owner's leg first, then went for the hand that lurched up from his owner's groin. He didn't scream, to his credit. He breathed hard and hissed and writhed and kicked at the dog, making contact once. When the dog went in again—this time for the throat—I grabbed the chain and yanked him back. He was still attacking. I stroked his back and his head; when that didn't work I pulled up on his chain until he started to sputter. He was growling—not at me but at the man huddled on the ground.

49

I looked at the man. His eyes were closed, his nose and mouth wounded. He might live, I thought, but for this they would put down the dog. I fiddled with the dog chain until it came off. I walked him a few paces, then smacked him hard on the backside so he would start running. I watched him go, his body flying over the grass and the sidewalk, his ears flapping in the street. When he had crossed, he slowed to a walk and did not look back, only wagged his tail as if to say, It's not so bad. I should thank you.

I walked into the diner as casually as I could, hoping I didn't have blood on me. The man's boss would come looking for him soon enough I thought, so I sat with my mother, who in a now-rare display of sentiment wrapped an arm around my shoulder and kissed my cheek. She said, "I got us stuffed pancakes," with an affection that made me wonder what happened to her while I was gone.

On the last leg of the trip, we began making ourselves presentable. We had the car washed and vacuumed, but we could not afford to repair the antenna or replace the broken window. We shook the dust out of our clothes and straightened up the last of our precious things and in so doing found, tucked safely in a depression under the mat in the backseat, my mother's old jewelry, which my father had said he pawned. We did laundry with the accumulated change of our trip, borrowing detergent from a college kid whose clothing was in as fragile condition as ours. To get our money's worth, my mother had me strip down to my underwear. Of course, nobody said a word—not with my mother watching, that sour expression on her face when she saw that my ribs were beginning to show. I kept my jacket on while I wormed out of my shirt. For warmth, I crouched by a dryer that had just been emptied, hugging my knees and making eye contact with no one.

We had been on the road for five weeks by then. Temperatures had dropped, and I assumed without having any proof that my father had frozen to death in a gutter somewhere, too drunk even to drag himself to shelter. We had long since gotten rid of his things—what little was left, anyway. When we first started living in the car, we sold most of our possessions, keeping only a few changes of clothes, toiletries, and cleaning products. In the beginning, I hid a few small trinkets in my underthings (toy weapons, various lock-and-key mechanisms), but my father found these and punished me for keeping them. By the time we left him, we had nothing of value to speak of and no reason to hold on to his memory. In his box of clothes, my mother found an envelope containing our birth certificates and their marriage license, which she tucked safely away and never spoke of again.

When we crossed the border into Oregon, our smiles cracked open over waterfalls, rivers, and lakes. I did not know how to drive, did not really understand roads or where Prospect was in relation to all this water, so every mile was the last and every turn, the one. We were driving with a borrowed sense of elation—forgetting that we still would not have any money, that I did not know anymore how to be a girl or how even to speak, and that our lives might not change for the better—when the car stalled. My mother sucked in one long breath, as though siphoning gas from a tank, and then broke down entirely.

I stepped out of the car. It smelled like too much frozen earth. When the door was closed, my mother's sobbing was muffled. I stayed close, drawing certainty from the sound. It was early, dark enough that I couldn't see my breath—certainly not as far as the next bend. I thought, Where are we? There was no light pollution. No one for miles, I realized. It would be at least an hour before a car drove past us and longer still before one stopped.

TWO LIES

One of the Lies I Tell My Children (#5)

If they do not clean their room, pretty soon it will be declared a health hazard and systems will be installed in and around the area to prevent the spread of slime mold from the air conditioner to the attic. In the mornings when they get dressed for school my children will have to pass through a decontamination chamber, where I will scrub them and disinfect them and where they will ask, in their weary voices, "Is this really necessary? The slime mold is our friend." At night, its black, iridescent fingers will feel around the surfaces of the room, eventually creeping its way onto their pillows and their sheets, and they will encourage it with the sugar water and the potato chips they deliberately smear over their faces. In the beginning, the slime mold will be wary of the offer and retreat every morning when the alarm goes off and I come knocking on their door; then gradually it will grow comfortable with the arrangement and grow stalks inside their nostrils, which will be jellied and metallic, giving the appearance of nose rings or other piercings. When summer arrives the children will have no reason to go outside and will hide in their room, feeding their new mold pet, giving it swaths and patches of their flesh for it to stretch out and grow spores. One day, the mold will take over, and what were once children will become host beds for the oozing, aromatic fungus creeping up between their toes; and because I love them and know how much they love to be dirty I will hook them up to saline drips with glucose and allow the mushrooms to grow in the recesses of their body. It will be a slow process, occurring gradually over weeks and months and necessitating a great deal of patience and understanding from me. Eventually, when school starts, my children will not be able to get out of bed, so I will stand over them, wishing I could see their hair under all the fungus. I will reach my hand out to stroke them, and in their strange unicellular way the slime molds will reach back, like flowers to the sun.

One of the Lies I Tell My Children (#27)

If they say they do not love me, I will have to get them a new mother who can satisfy all their expectations. This new mother will be younger, thinner, and kinder and will most likely be better in the kitchen than I am or have ever professed to be. In fact, this new mother will spend so much time cooking and cleaning that she won't be able to keep a job, which means she will either have to be independently wealthy or marry rich in order to provide for them. In any case, I see a father in their future. He will be a lawyer and a businessman, something with a tailored suit that says he is important and professional, the sort of man who will roll up his sleeves and drag his arm through the gutter when he feels it's going to rain. My children will look up to this man, and he will teach them how to clean their rooms and do their homework, using positive reinforcement if they grow sullen or wistful—if, for instance, they remember that they had another father figure once, and he was an engine mechanic and a sculptor who liked to work with metal. This new man in their lives will of course know all about the old one, and he will do his best to steer them away from any memories of their former family or the accident. He will know that they were little then, and that I had to explain it to them with a story, saying, "If your father never comes back, then we will do the best we can," and pray they understood. Their new parents will never have to lie to them like this. They will be happy and healthy, and when my children see me through the window their new parents will say, "Oh, don't mind her. She's just a crazy lady going through the garbage," but by then my children will be kind, and they will help me through my struggles, bringing me food sometimes—a banana, a grape—and asking me, "Why are you crying? It's a lovely day." There will be no answer to this, except to say yes, yes, it is a lovely day. I'm sorry I frightened you.

GENERAL, MINISTER, HORSE, CANNON

"Call me Theta," he said. "Use the symbol, like a mathematician; my people should know that I'm good at math." Θ was fourteen years old. Like most tenth graders in his school, he was in trigonometry that year, and though he always excelled in math he found most of his classes dull and tedious. His teachers plodded along at a speed that bored him and led him to daydream about utilizing his brain for something grander, something historic: the invention of a star destroyer, for instance, or a cold fusion reactor, which he would then use to monopolize the energy industry, making himself rich. It was on the bus ride home, while talking to a friend, the girl who lived just across the street, that he hit upon the Great Idea: "I shall become Emperor." When she asked him of what, he said, "Of the world, of course."

"Not the galaxy?"

He paused, disappointed that he had not thought of this himself. "Good point."

She nodded, thinking this the end of the discussion, and turned once again to the window, forehead lolling against the glass as she stared blankly at the road. Now and then, the bus lurched forward suddenly, and her head lifted just enough to avoid being bumped. It disturbed him to see this; he always forgot how much it disturbed him. She sat in silence while his lips moved swiftly, nervously, their thin lines forming words that laid out his plans for world domination. It was all so clear to him then, clear and colorless, like a battle plan drawn on a thick sheet of glass.

"You will write my autobiography."

She peered at him quizzically. "Shouldn't you write that yourself?"

"I cannot. English is not my native tongue." His English had never been as muscular or as supple as he would have liked. He considered this his greatest failing and cursed the demons in him that led him to believe, when he was growing up in China, that he needed only learn the ABCs in order to pass elementary school. After failing English in sixth grade, he spent five months poring over his workbooks, examining every word, every semicolon; but by the time he caught up to the rest of the class it was too late. He couldn't teach his mouth to make new sounds without hearing the old ones. He had since become self-conscious of his accent—the boxiness of it. He often wished he could speak with the precision of his friend, whom he had seen reading books alone in the cafeteria—books that were not assigned for class. He was impressed by his friend's ability to make sense of the convolutions of the English language. If only his autobiography could be written in Chinese, he thought; but, alas, his American subjects wouldn't read it. "I need a real writer. My people will want to hear my story."

"Your propaganda, you mean."

His face split into a grin. "I knew you would understand."

She shut her eyes, laughing to herself. She was still leaning against the window, hunching like a beggar against the chill. Her shirt sagged, ballooning around her chest and doing her no favors, physically speaking. Her clothes were all several sizes too large, and whenever he saw her in the halls at school it appeared as if she were shrinking inside of them, as if, by the end of the hallway, she would disappear entirely. When she retreated deeper into her corner, gazing at the telephone wires listlessly, helplessly, he frowned and asked if she was okay. "Fine. Just bored is all. We've been sitting here for almost thirty minutes."

It couldn't be helped. Northern Virginia was rapidly becoming a suburb of DC, and, that far out, past Manassas and the Prince William Parkway, roads weren't built to sustain the comings and goings of another city's workforce. There was one two-lane road, and it invariably turned what should've been a quick and easy thirteen miles into a long crawl to school. On mornings like that one, the bus sat in traffic under the shade of trees whose branches tapped the roof and rustled just outside of the windows. There was no radio and only just enough heat, and the driver's daughter was asleep in the seat in front of them; they tried not to wake her with this talk of a book.

"I will provide the necessary equations."

"What do equations have to do with your life story?"

"Math is essential to understanding my ballistic missile program."

"Are you sure you want to share that information? Your enemies could use it."

He tilted his head, lifting one finger to shake at her. "Very good. You passed the test."

Again she shook her head, charmed by this adolescent arrogance, which paradoxically led him to hold her in high regard, almost like an equal. This was why he had chosen her: because he would never allow someone with an inferior intellect to ghostwrite his autobiography. He would think that insulting not just to his legacy but also to her and her talents as a writer. If she hadn't known this, she may well have taken offense at the condescension of his tests, which took the form of puzzles, riddles, and strategy games, like the one where they played chess in their heads, moving pieces on a small imaginary board until one of them lost track of a pawn and made a fatal mistake. All things considered, they were pretty evenly matched.

*   *   *

That winter, on the long, dark bus rides to school, he taught her Chinese chess, knowing that by spring she would understand the strategy so thoroughly as to beat him about half the time; that was why he taught her. In order to play, they would turn to face each other, laying a two-inch binder flat between them, then unfolding the board over it. It was a cheap board, just a sheet of plastic with the lines painted on, and the pieces were thick round tiles like hockey pucks demarcating their rank with Chinese characters: general, minister, horse, cannon. When placed on the grid, the tiles occupied corners and intersections. To win, a player had to defeat the other's army and capture the opposing general. Taking pieces meant violently overrunning their positions; this was the best part, they agreed. Θ laughed savagely when she barreled a cannon across the board, knocking his last soldier clear off the binder and smacking him squarely on the wrist with it. His sharp teeth glinted as he said, "So, the pupil has become the master."

She snorted. Her stomach rumbled, its cries like the gurgling of a dying man.

"Breakfast is the most important meal of the day," he said, tapping his temple importantly while she mumbled that they'd run out of cereal that morning. "Great minds like ours cannot go to waste." Her play had become erratic, unfocused, and when the boy in the seat behind them began unwrapping a granola bar her entire body went still with want. Seeing this, Θ quickly changed the subject. "My grandfather and I used to play chess," he said. "He had a beautiful set."

She watched him trace the edges of the board. "Was it made out of marble?"

He shook his head. "Stone. Each piece was," he said, weighing a tile in his palm, "at least three times as heavy as this." When she extended her hand, he let it fall like water into her palm.

She closed her fist, lifting the piece up and down. "Is he still in China?"

He nodded. His grandfather lived in the city where Θ was born: Jinan, the City of Springs, capital of Shandong Province. He took great pains describing its glory to her. It had seventy-two, yes, seventy-two natural springs, each of which had provided inspiration to a great Chinese author at one point or another; the most notable of these writers was Lao She. "Hold on." Θ was attempting to translate one of Lao She's lovely verses in his head: the capital had "three sides surrounded by mountains, and one side by water, of a mountain view, and half a city of lakes."

Θ was deeply unsatisfied with the translation. He allowed himself a minute of sourness, just thinking about how English could sap the beauty out of Chinese poetry, then broke into an exuberant grin, because this was all great material for his biography. It would begin with his birth: Θ was born July 8, 1988. Of this birth, his mother was known to say, "I knew you were a boy from the vehemence of your cries." He was proud of this story. When he recounted it, his expression was gleeful, his voice excited, and his friend had to remind him of the sleeping child in the front seat.

Θ nodded rapidly. "You should take out a sheet of paper," he whispered. "To take notes."

He waited until she was ready, then began:

"We lived in perfect happiness. Three years, perfect happiness. My mother, my biological father, and me. Then we discovered what kind of man he really was. We'd believed him when he said he was going on business trips." He was a businessman, but, as it turned out, these trips were just the legs of an extensive drug-trafficking operation of the kind that results in an extended prison sentence for anyone involved.

"How long was he sent away for?"

On this, as on many other things, Θ hedged the truth, aware that it could reflect poorly on him. He said only that his biological father had been sent away for a very long time. "If he's ever released, I will be old when it happens."

"That doesn't clarify anything. Yesterday you called Mrs. Wheeler old, and she's twenty-six!"

He lifted his head proudly. "When I'm twenty-six, I will be Emperor."

"Yeah," she said, shaking her head as she looked away. She considered his reflection in the window a moment before asking if he ever visited his biological father in prison.

He nodded curtly. "Twice a year. My mother insisted." He would not have gone there otherwise. He despised the man and had no qualms saying so. He made it very clear that in the book of his life she was not to write off any of his successes as an attempt to escape comparison with that terrible criminal.

It was true: He had always striven to be the best. The top of his class. Teacher's pet. When he was in first grade, he was so beloved that he was granted the privilege of helping grade his fellow students' exams—their math exams, to be specific. Even then, everyone knew that he was very proud of being very good at math, which only made him relish this grading process all the more. Back then, his teacher used thin, thin rice paper, and it often tore under the force of his pen when he marked a paper with a bad grade. He loved to see the others fail; and yet he was permitted to continue.

Or, at least, he was for a time. There was some competition. Some fighting. Eventually, he realized that his arms could extend his attack range—and his legs could extend it farther still. He liked to get into scrapes with other boys. He had a rival at the age of eight: Deng-yi-da, a boy in his fourth-grade class. They were the top two students and were constantly warring for the number one spot. Whenever the teacher asked a question, the two would fly out of their seats, raising their hands as high as they could, trying to make themselves taller, faster, smarter, but to no avail. That was the only year they had class together. In fifth grade Θ did well, though his new teacher didn't emphasize math and science, but in sixth grade he failed English again, and in seventh grade he moved to America. He had not seen his biological father since.

His mother remarried not long after they emigrated. Θ remembers a brief period of time in which he resented her for marrying this man (this utter stranger), who like all men at that point in Θ's life seemed like nothing more than a placeholder for a coming disaster. Θ prepared himself to be disappointed. He waited every day for this new man to reveal himself as ugly, mean, criminal, and a danger to Θ's future, but instead of falling apart their lives grew better— their house bigger, his mother happier—and finally he had to look at the stranger and reassess. He was Chinese, too, though born in America and capable of speaking English with no discernable accent. He was and had been for some time a rather successful lawyer and expressed a careful, measurable interest in Θ that at first seemed too deliberate, but after some consideration proved only respectful.

"Don't refer to him as my stepfather," he told his friend one icy winter morning when he found himself dwelling on the extent of his fortune. "He's not my *stepfather*; he's my father. He raised me. I can only hope to someday be as good as him."

His friend agreed. "Do you want to be a lawyer like him?"

Θ had considered it before, though it wasn't expected of him (he made that point clear). "I think I'll study some law," he said, "along with ethics and philosophy. To be a really great leader, I must have a strong sense of justice. Otherwise my people will not love me."

"But if they're afraid of you they'll still obey you."

"Fear can be useful," he admitted. Sometimes Θ thought it was the only way to dominate. When she pressed him, he told her that most of his plans for world domination involved violence of some sort. A struggle, a display of power to quell the forces of his enemies. In these scenarios, he always had enemies. He always defeated them (one way or another), but the fact that he had to and even seemed to want to worried Θ. He sensed that there was a part of him that was capable of unspeakable cruelty, just as there was a part of him that operated with a godlike beneficence, and it struck him one day that his friend was probably the only person in the world who knew him for both sides of his personality. He felt understood, but also, in some ways, frightened. She was like a well in danger of drying up, and whenever he dropped his secrets into her he listened to be sure that there was still something on the receiving end; that it wasn't hollow, all the things they said.

*   *   *

More and more she seemed to go to school hungry. It had occurred to him before that she might be starving herself. He knew all the warning signs of anorexia: the headaches, the lethargy, the negative body image. She often referred to herself as fat in a voice that made him look her up and down and say very flatly that she was not. Her clothes just didn't flatter her figure, and it was this fact, more than any other, that gave Θ pause: because these clothes must have fit, once, months or maybe even years before, when she was thirty, forty, fifty pounds heavier—and feeling it. Even now, she carried herself like someone who had absolutely no idea what her body looked like. She was just so *hungry*, he thought, and maybe that was why he asked her if she wanted to join him in the cafeteria for breakfast.

"I don't have any money," she said.

He shook his head gently. "No problem. Pick whatever you like."

She grabbed applesauce, milk, a breakfast sandwich made with something like a biscuit.

He felt a certain pride, knowing that he'd provided for her this way. Even before they sat, Θ knew he would buy her breakfast from then on. She inhaled the food, hunching over the tray as if afraid it would be taken away from her, like kindness. She dipped her head when he chided, "Chew your food. It takes twenty minutes for the stomach to relay a message that it is full."

She tried to change the subject by saying, "I have a geometry test today."

He frowned. "Why are you still in geometry? You should be in trigonometry."

"Trig wasn't a separate class at my old school, so I wasn't on track to take it."

"Right," he said, though he had forgotten that she moved. Somehow, the facts of her history always eluded him, and he struggled to remember where she lived before. She was a blank that way, a kind of empty book in which he dared not write.

"I was at Westfield. It's in another county, so the system is different. I'm teaching myself trig so I can catch up. At the end of the year, they're going to give me a test, and if I pass I get to skip ahead to calculus." Of course, she would pass easily; there was no doubt in his mind. It was smart of her just to arrange it, and when the bell rang he realized they would get to take calculus together. They could be study partners. It was unfortunate that they didn't have a class together already and that, at the end of the day, he went to his house and she to hers. He never thought about inviting her over; they weren't friends like that. When Θ was home, he was home. It was that simple. He sat at his computer. He studied, and after dinner he played chess with his father (who always beat him, though never by much). In all this there was no time to think that he might miss her. Sometimes, at night, he saw a light shining inside her house, where the windows had no shades, no blinds, or curtains, and he could see right through to what could be a dining room maybe, or a nice room for entertaining guests. He wasn't sure; he wasn't an interior designer. Even so, it struck him as odd that all the rooms stood empty. Completely empty, but for the light.

What goes on in that hollow house, he asked himself. Never out loud. Just in his head.

One day his mother witnessed his friend's parents breaking into their car. That ugly white van of theirs. Evidently, they had locked themselves out. Her father had to take a rock and smash one of the back windows. Θ mentioned this to his friend the next morning. "And your mother just stood there," he said. "Laughing at him."

She snorted, "That woman is not my mother."

Her vehemence surprised him. "Who is she?"

"A whore," she said, and her voice knocked the breath out of him. He'd never seen her so mad. He felt almost as if he had never seen her at all. But then she relented. "Her name's Manuela. She's my stepmother."

Manuela. He had never heard that name before.

"She's from Ecuador. They met online."

"They got married without ever seeing each other?"

"No, he visited her in Quito. He was there for two weeks."

"Who took care of you?"

"He left me with my grandmother," she said, and there was a long enough pause after this for Θ to think she wasn't going to elaborate, but then she did. She told him it was in midsummer. A warm couple of weeks in July. She spent a lot of time fanning herself out in the gazebo. Θ likes the word. "Gazebo." G-a-z-e-b-o, a roofed structure built with lattices and pine offering up a fine view of the backyard, with its lush grass and giant willow trees. She used it in a sentence: "Every Easter Grandma hid a couple eggs under the gazebo. Plastic eggs," she said. "Not real ones."

Θ appreciated her finally opening up to him, though he knew she was only telling him this to stave off the inevitable question: her mother. "Where is she?"

"She died. Cancer. I was twelve."

He wanted to ask what kind of cancer, when was she diagnosed, did she suffer terribly, but when he opened his mouth what came out was: "I'm sorry."

She said nothing. There was nothing to say.

And despite all this new information Θ felt as though he knew nothing about her family or her home life. On the few instances when they did discuss something personal, it always came as a shock to him, as if she'd just dropped a little monster into his hands and expected him to talk to it like it was perfectly normal. What surprised him most was the fact that he could—that he could change subjects in the course of a sentence, that he could bear to think of her in pain.

Some shocks were more painful than others. Like one afternoon, when he was headed for their bus and happened to spy his friend standing off to one side, talking to a woman. A stranger. This woman clearly wasn't a teacher, but she didn't look like a student. She was older but shorter than his friend and also better dressed. The woman handed her a bag of Taco Bell; then the bus started to pull out, and his friend rushed on at the last second, leaving the woman standing alone.

"That's my sister," his friend said, already digging in to her food.

He caught one last glimpse of the woman. "She looks nothing like you."

His friend nodded, wiping her lips of grease. "She's my half sister. My mother's side."

"Why did she come to see you at school?"

"My dad doesn't let me see her."

"Why?"

"He's ashamed."

Of what, she didn't say. That left Θ to fill in the blanks.

Ashamed, he repeated in his head, trying to suss out the word's various connotations. He knew a couple things about shame. He felt it daily, acutely, as he did his homework and studied and studied some more, all to reduce the chances of failure. He couldn't fail. He couldn't bear for anyone to see the true extent of his weakness. His shortcomings. His stupidity. Perhaps that was what her father was afraid of: the things other people knew, things he couldn't change about the world or about himself. Shame like that could tear families apart.

Sometimes Θ had to admit that life wasn't perfect. That in fact he was not doing as well in school as he could or should be, that actually his mother rode him about his grades every day and that their relationship had gradually deteriorated as he'd grown older. In his darkest moments, he thought of China, of those last days in Jinan and how hard he had railed against her. He remembered thinking she was ruining his life. And what did life mean to him, then? Water—the many streams of it—his reflection as he walked along the edge of a lake with his grandfather on a gray afternoon not long before they moved to America. Somehow, Θ had gotten it in his head that if he left he would never return. He would never see China again, and then one day he would forget the sound of the Black Tiger Spring drowning out his mother's warning and the terror he felt when he dove into the Five Dragon Pool and the water flexed around him like a muscle. How could the waters in America ever live up to such an experience? Everything had been so immediate then. Now, he sat in his bedroom and contemplated polite ways of subverting his mother's power over him, and that was what he called a day.

In the spring, Θ's grandfather came for an extended visit. His grandfather's presence so consumed his every thought he had trouble focusing on anything else; the seven hours he spent at school each day passed him in a blur, and it wasn't until he floated onto the bus back home that the world started to regain definition. He remembered these rides as being short and loud, the seats sticky, ready to burst. Outside, the lives of others seemed to Θ vigorous and unremarkable, and it was only with extraordinary effort that he was able to hold up his side of the conversation as he and his friend walked home.

One day was like any other day: they parted at the corner, each to their own houses, and Θ forgot her as soon as she walked through her front door. He and his grandfather had plans to play Go, and this required Θ's undivided attention. His grandfather was a grand master, a player whose moves dictated his opponent's, demanding immediate responses that made long-term strategizing near impossible. Θ had never beaten his grandfather. Never come close, even, though he felt no shame in his failure. In the back of his mind, Θ knew, his brain was sifting through dozens of hours of game play, searching for patterns, unlocking his grandfather's secrets, and someday it would finish its analysis and he would win. When he grew frustrated, it was only because of the sluggish pace of his education. He longed for the day when he could anticipate problems before they arose.

Near the end of the game, Θ's mother pulled him aside. "The girl across the street is sitting on her front step," she said. "She's been there for over an hour and hasn't gone inside."

Θ remained calm. He placed his stone on the grid, begged forgiveness of his grandfather, and climbed the stairs at a normal, even pace. He hadn't realized that it was such a chilly day, but it hit him as soon as he walked outside. He went alone but knew without having to look back that his mother was stationed at the window, eyes fixed on his back as he ambled down the driveway. Once he realized his friend wouldn't come when called he took his time, slipped his hand into his pocket as he considered what to do. It was cold. The wind was whipping her hair around, making it look like snakes. She must be freezing, he thought.

When he was close enough, she stared up at him miserably. "I lost my key."

"You could have knocked on my door."

"I'm not allowed."

He frowned. He felt, somehow, judged. "Come inside."

"What if my father comes home?"

"I will leave a note." This process took a few minutes: they first had to find tape, and then they had to walk back across the street, and, the whole time, she had this frenzied look about her, as if she expected her father to come screeching around the corner and smack her in the face.

Θ made introductions between his friend, his mother, and his grandfather. He then offered her snacks and asked if she would like to play Ping-Pong. She neither accepted nor declined, only stood there, raking her fingers through her frazzled, windswept hair. He led her downstairs to the game room, where she hovered next to the Ping-Pong table, listening for the doorbell. He offered her a paddle, but she was still shaking from the cold.

His mother went upstairs to make her a cup of tea.

His grandfather chattered kindly at her in Chinese.

Soon enough there was a knock at the front door.

Her father was not quite what Θ expected: he was older than he seemed from afar, for one thing, or perhaps he just looked that way because the skin of his neck had begun to sag, giving him a jowl. He walked into the house with his head held high like a turkey and his blue eyes opened wide, as if startled. He looked at his daughter then and clearly didn't believe a word she said about losing the key and getting locked out. Θ tried making a joke about how she refused to play Ping-Pong because she was too afraid of losing, but the man didn't understand. Certainly he didn't laugh.

After, Θ's mother commented on how rude the man was. How rude they both were.

Θ said nothing. But first thing the next morning he asked his friend what happened. It was silly, really: she lost her house key, left it with her gym lock on a bench in the locker room after PE. It was an accident, nothing more.

"Why does he hold that against you?"

"He thinks I gave the key to my sister to be copied."

"Why would you do that?"

"I didn't."

"I know, but why would he think you would?"

She lifted her shoulders in a weary shrug. "I don't know what goes on in his head."

Something must've gone wrong with his logic, Θ thought. It was the only explanation. In his free time, Θ started running little simulations, trying to understand the mind of a man who honestly believed his friend would do such a thing, as if that was even a thing one would do: give away a key to be copied by someone. Only thieves snuck into houses that way, and for her to be a thief required there to be something worth stealing in that big, empty house. Something else, then. Something less sinister. What is a key? Just the ability to enter. So perhaps what her father feared was less the taking away and more the letting in of memory, of the past, and of all the things he had to be ashamed of, of which her sister was the biggest one.

Half sister, he remembered. That seemed important.

It didn't surprise him that his friend never spoke of the incident again. There were always other, newer problems, their intricacies requiring all her attention and energy just to manage. She became careful to the point of being calculating. She saw her sister every week (or nearly so) and worked very hard at not getting caught. Still, there were a few close calls. Like the time her sister picked her up from school with the idea that they would drive behind the bus and have a chance to talk for once; only they took a detour to get some fast food and got caught in traffic, and when she was dropped off she had no idea whether the bus had already gone and whether her father was home and watching to see that she arrived at the same time as all the other kids. Or like that time they got off the bus one afternoon and Θ pointed to a white van parked on the corner and said, "Isn't that your dad?" And, sure enough, her father was sitting there, watching her. She hung back with Θ a moment, then approached carefully, leaning over to speak to her father through the open window. He must've told her to get in, because she did so immediately, and Θ watched as the van made a U-turn and sped up the road toward the house. He never asked why her father was waiting there. He already knew.

It went on like this for months. The weather warmed. The school year ended. Summer was free and clear, and it wasn't until she showed up on his doorstep, a few weeks into break, that he started to worry. He was not expecting her. It alarmed him that he hadn't been thinking of her until that moment and that he never made plans to see her before. He feared something had happened. She was standing there, looking thinner, paler, asking to come in, even though they both knew it was against the rules. Her father wasn't home, she said. He wouldn't be back for hours.

Still, Θ didn't relax. "I thought he took away your key privileges."

She shrugged. "I left the door unlocked."

He raised his eyebrows but still invited her inside. He knew even before they sat down in the kitchen that his mother was going to come downstairs. That she was going to be furious with him, but that her reputation as a hostess would force her to be civil and offer his friend snacks. She would smile at them, thinking this was enough, and then, when the plates were ready and the soda had been poured, she would ask the inevitable, "Where's your father?"

And then: "Where does he work?"

"Safeway. He's a stock boy."

Here, his mother's smile fell. She didn't know the meaning of the term "stock boy," but she knew it wasn't a "manager" or "owner" or anything respectable like that. In Chinese, she asked Θ a series of questions, wondering what kind of money he could be making and how he was paying for that big house and if the wife worked—because it seemed to her that the woman never lifted a finger. He did not know how to translate all this, so when his friend asked him what his mother was saying he shook his head softly and asked only if she wanted to play Chinese chess. He went upstairs to get the board, and when he came back his mother was gone and the sandwiches had all been eaten. Without asking if his friend was still hungry, he brought her a bag of pita chips and a glass of water. He suspected that this was the last time he would see her.

It didn't surprise him when he lost the first game. He blinked at the grid a few times, then accepted defeat. While he set up the board for another game, she asked him, "When you rule the world, what will your mandate be? Presume for the sake of the exercise that you won't be an evil dictator. Think beloved."

And he did think about it. He said, "Well—I'll destroy drugs." That was first. Then came water—clean water, drinking water. The world was in dire need of it, and Jinan could deliver. He planned to rule from his home-land, he said. She knew what a joy that would be for him. On clear days, he should be able to see his entire kingdom reflected in the surface of a single lake. How to describe its beauty, and where even to begin? There was so much. Sky. Its three sides surrounded by mountains, and then by water. Up ahead, a golden sculpture of the Buddha glinting in the sun. In his mind, Θ could see it all. He stood under the pavilion to watch as the light turned the water a glorious shade of green. That was the version of Θ she would always remember: the teenage boy. The square face. The accent that would never go away—and that smile. They used to sit together on the bus. They laughed. He always forgot how much they laughed.

THE ITHACA MOMENT

Cornell. The bitter cold. You've never forgotten. You were just eighteen when you felt its teeth the first time. It rolled in through the window like a dense fog and sucked all the heat from between your legs. Your lover had come and gone, but there would be another one, then another, until finally one stuck. She was a fifth-year grad student. Nine years older. She shopped at the co-op and ate melon balls wrapped in prosciutto until you could taste it about her: how she turned your flesh into pulp, how she left salt in places you never wanted it. Sometimes, she made you cry in bed.

That was junior year. You were different then. Gentler, and with a little padding. You had a habit of falling down, falling hard. You bruised your hip during an ice storm that swept up Gun Hill while you were leaving her apartment, and you couldn't help thinking it was a bad omen. When you flew home to Virginia for winter break, the memory of her lingered in your skin, making you itch. You tried everything to take your mind off her: reading, ignoring your family, obsessively checking for your grades—until finally they came in the day before Christmas and you found yourself with nothing to do, because you'd read all your books and your mom had her own life. You remember hopping on your bike. Hitting all your old haunts. You missed the smell of pine and sawdust at Home Depot; the scent is thick and clean, and you hold it in your lungs as you walk back into the cold Virginia air. It's warm compared to Ithaca. This would be considered T-shirt weather in Upstate New York. The frat boys would be out playing ultimate Frisbee. You'd run into almost everyone you know on campus. But she wouldn't text you back.

One day, you ride your bike down to the abandoned elementary school to see the netless basketball hoops, the broken swings, and the jungle gym. A guy you knew from high school is there: alone, skulking around a corner. Eli, his name is. When he recognizes you, his eyebrows shoot higher than you thought they could go; perhaps this is why you hesitate. You knew his face when it was thinner. You're still holding on to an image of him as a track star, not winning the big race, but floundering around afterward, trying to sit down, while his limbs refuse to cooperate. Eli was the boy you lost your virginity to freshman year, and you remember clinging to his hard, warm shoulder blades as he climaxed. But these things have nothing to do with the man in front of you. His nod is different. He's baffled by your sudden appearance.

He hustles forward, squeezing his shoulders in the cold. "Hey. What are you doing here?"

"I was just going for a ride." You float a wrist in the direction of your bike, which you've left unlocked near the basketball hoop across the court. He looks at you, not the bike; he knows it's there. "What about you?"

"Oh, nothing," he says, the word sliding around like a hand over still water. He glances at the far corner of the blacktop where you came from. Then at the corner he came from. Then you again, and with a different kind of anxiety. "Just meeting someone."

"A friend?" He answers yes too quickly. You let it slide. "So do you hang out here a lot?"

"Sometimes. It's quiet. Good for a game of pickup." As he says this he pretends to shoot a basketball, but his form is sloppy, no follow-through, and you can tell that even his imagination doesn't allow him to sink that shot. His shoulders droop. He knows you're not fooled.

But you give him a way out: "Want to play?"

He regards you with skepticism. He points out that you don't have a ball, and he lifts one eyebrow when you say you don't need one. His eyes follow your motions, bobbing as you begin to dribble, first with one hand, then two. You go slow, so he gets it. He nods then. When he takes his hand from his pocket, you stop dribbling. His eyes are on the imaginary ball you hold to your chest, and that's a mistake, because if he could see the grin that spreads over your face, then he'd be prepared when you snap the ball at his head.

He flinches. For a split second, your open palms are flying right at him, and he rears back before he can help himself. Then he snatches the ball out of the air over his left ear, and this stops you from laughing. You get out one bright, self-satisfied huff. Then he bounces the ball lightly to you, and the game begins.

Neither of you is very good. You try to maneuver around each other, but keeping track of the ball's logical trajectory is too much, and it messes with your footwork. Every so often, one of you manages to break away for a layup, but you both have to agree you don't make many of those. Just once, you pull a smooth, long three-point shot, and he whistles as he traces the arc. He steps up his game after that. It's your possession. He's all over you, and you get mired midcourt, trying to protect the ball by turning your back to him. You're stuck. He's got these long arms and they won't let you go anywhere. You go one way and then the other, but you end up just gyrating in place. He laughs and smacks the ball away for an easy two points. He has a truly embarrassing victory dance you try not to watch.

You wipe the sweat from your forehead. Too late, you think to put your hair up. You have a hair tie in your mouth, and that's why you have a hard time telling him, at first, about the obvious bulge in his jeans. You glance at his crotch a few times so he gets it. When he does, he looks down and says, "Oh. Sorry."

You take the hair tie from your mouth but say nothing.

He begins to say, "I'll just—" But you put up your hand, telling him to do what he needs to. He tucks it under his belt as you tie your hair. When he's done, he wiggles, then says, "It's as uncomfortable for me as it is for you."

You shrug. "I'm fine. It's your problem, not mine."

"Well, you're not the one who has to deal with blue balls."

You give him a look of exaggerated pity. "That's not a thing."

"I know. I was just kidding."

"If you say so." The taunt draws an indignant sigh from him, and that draws a laugh from you. You are finding this all terribly amusing, more than you should, and more than he's ready to forgive you for, apparently. He starts to sulk. He slouches over to his backpack, the same kind of pouch drawstring he wore in high school. He roots around in it for his cellphone, then stares at the screen for a while. You say, "Is your friend coming?"

"What? No." He shrugs. "It's just a girl."

"Oh, I see."

"It's not what you think." He flashes her picture for you.

"It's exactly what I think."

He wobbles his head, fake laughing.

"She doesn't look like your type," you say. She's hooded and smoking.

He scowls, "What do you know about my type?"

You click your tongue against your teeth, but when you start to make a snide comment, you find you have nothing, so that's what you say: "Nothing. I have no idea what you do these days."

This isn't the answer he wants. He drops his phone into the pouch and cinches it.

When you suggest a rematch, he grimaces. You roll your eyes. "Still?"

He draws himself up, putting on airs. "I am a young man in the prime of my life."

"Gross."

"Jesus," he says, deflating. "That was a long time ago."

You saunter over, whispering. "You mean you don't want me to finish you off?"

"Are you offering?" After he says this, he drops his hands into his coat pockets and cocks his head, as if to say, Now we can put all this silliness to an end. And he jumps (visibly jumps) as in one smooth motion you hike back the sleeve of your sweatshirt and find him. This part is easy. You aren't teenagers, this isn't high school, and you know what you're doing. You apply enough pressure at the start to make him docile. You watch his face. You see it: that little flip in his eyes, what takes his surprise and reroutes it through adrenaline and pleasure until it ends up altogether different. His mouth opens. He adjusts to give you space. You feel a certain tenderness then. You ease up, and he likes this friction better. He pulls you toward him, pulls up, because he's taller by a few inches, two or three. Your toes lift off the ground. His thigh sneaks between yours but doesn't press. You throw an arm around his neck (cling there) as he tucks his hands up under all three layers of your clothes. The cold air shouldn't startle you, but it does. You thought he would go right for your breasts. And when it's that close, he does finally cup them; but for the longest time, you just hold each other up, as in a hug.

As he sets you down, you feel wrung out. You miss the heat of his neck and want to cry.

He doesn't notice. He takes a moment. "Did I get any on you?"

You twist around just enough for him to check. Nothing.

He rubs his hands over his red cheeks. He says, "It's too cold to be outside." Then he looks at you a moment before he asks if you want to come over.

You shake your head slowly. "Can we just go for a ride instead?"

"Sure." He pauses. His gaze isn't on you. "We'll have to get the car."

You fetch your bike. You hop on but don't ride, just pedal slow enough that he can jog along beside you. There's something of his old form in this. You remember he graduated with a track scholarship to an even better Ivy. You remember he lost it, but not why. You want to ask but think better of it. You focus on maintaining your balance as you tackle dirt roads and cut across the backyard of someone you don't even know.

He says, "Do you know where we're going?"

"I assumed we were going to your mother's house." Neither of you stops, but you do look over your shoulder, briefly, wondering if you guessed correctly. "This is the way, right?"

He stares down at the handlebars, avoiding your gaze. "Yeah, it's just up ahead."

It's late afternoon. You figure there's an hour, maybe an hour and a half of light left. Overhead, the sun has started moving toward the horizon, but the clouds are so gray it's hard to be sure. "Looks like snow," he says, but it doesn't smell like it to you. If anything, you think it'll rain. His house as you approach seems gray, lifeless.

"My mother isn't home," he says.

You think he might try to invite you inside again, but he doesn't, and he doesn't in a way that makes you think, Yeah, she's home. He stands at the rear of the truck (the same one he drove in high school). You ask him if the bike rack is new. It isn't.

Inside, you wait for the truck to warm. He says, "You're at Cornell, right?"

"Yeah, I'm just here for Christmas."

"So, you like it up there?" You take too long to answer, and he snorts. "Yeah, so, that's a no," he says, then turns around to check if he's clear. He keeps a hand behind your headrest for an element of stability. Even so, he doesn't look at you.

You say, "I don't hate it."

"Suuuure."

"I don't. I just don't know what good it's doing me."

He is quiet, at ease. He thinks a moment. "Aren't you getting your money's worth?"

"It's not about that."

He shrugs. "Well, I guess it's your parents' money."

"Jesus," you say, and by the self-satisfied look on his face you realize he got you.

He turns right, toward the river. "Let's go to that picnic spot. It's your favorite, right?"

This seems weird to you. You say, "It's a lot of people's favorite."

"Yeah, but I remember you used to go down there all the time with Lilies B. and T."

"That's true." You haven't thought about that in a long time, but you guess there isn't any reason to, since you're not really friends with them anymore and that one night wasn't even the first time you kissed a girl. You turn to him. "Do you know if they're still around?"

"I see Lily B. around sometimes. She works at the Food Lion."

"That's right. She was going to be assistant manager." You remember her saying it, then find it sad that this is one of the few examples you have left of her voice. You used to know it so well. That seems like years ago. You count: one, two, three.

It isn't a long drive—only a few miles. When you arrive at the site, there's some evidence of a recent cook fire, but no one's around that you can see. A car passes by. A deer safely crosses the road. You are otherwise alone. He seems to want to sit at the benches, but you pick a path out over the rocks on the shore. At its very edges, the river is still frozen from the nightly temperature dip, and this makes you think of cracking an ice tray, of glass. The little floe gives at the slightest touch of your finger. Eli pokes it with his toe, and this act completely submerges the ice, so that it begins to melt. He kicks a stone into the water, where the current bears it sluggishly along. He looks somehow disappointed.

You stare downriver toward the bend. You're aware of him watching. He wants you to make the first move, but he doesn't mind drawing you out if he has to.

"You're shivering," he says.

You press your lips into the warmth of your knee.

"I have a blanket in the truck."

"I'm fine."

"You sure?"

You nod yes. You don't bother to shrug off his concerned touch.

He goes to fetch the blanket. You listen to his sounds: the scratch of his hand drawn over his stubble, the weight of his boot on frosted grass, then gravel, then silence, before the release of the lock, the catch of it. He takes his time shaking the blanket out. When he comes back, he has it wrapped around his shoulders. He sits so close your thighs touch. He seems in good spirits. "So," he says. "Tell me about Ithaca."

This is the last thing you want to do. You've been avoiding the place in your mind, trying to hold the undeniable fact of it at bay with some success. Every so often, you get a flash, a brief window into your life. You see your room. You spend a lot of time alone there. She rarely invites you to her place but you waste most nights in hopes that she will. You wait for her call. At dawn, you're still waiting as light breaks over the clock tower, tumbles down the Slope, and hits you in the face. You rush to class. You have four in a row and end up feeling pummeled. You think you might drop out, but you can't tell him this. You can't tell anyone. You say only that Ithaca is very nice. It has a lot of natural beauty. You tell him about the gorges, the orchards, the annual Apple Harvest Festival. You shrug. You guess it's like any college town.

"Well, obviously. But what do people do there?"

You frown at his tone. "What did you do when you went away to college?"

He snorts at your attempted insult, then tells the truth: "I fucked around."

"Is that it?"

"That's it," he says, reinforcing each word with a sharp nod. "I lost it. I was always either too drunk or too high to run. An athlete has to stay competitive."

"Are you still doing drugs?"

"No." He says this clearly, simply. You believe him.

"That's good," you say.

He nods like someone who has to say this to himself regularly, but a little twitch makes him shrug, too. "I smoke sometimes. Not often." He glances behind him and then pulls one string of his pack down over his shoulder. "I have some here if you want it."

"No thanks. I'm not buying."

His laugh is sudden, short, and not really a laugh. "Yeah, I got that."

"How much you got there?" You lean over for a peek, but he pulls the bag away.

"None of your business."

"Oh, I see."

He doesn't like that at all, and he draws the strings taut before setting the pouch aside. He wants to change the subject. You can tell. He thrusts his legs out in front of him and tilts his head back, regarding the cloudy and ever-darkening sky.

You tell him it's snowing up in Ithaca.

He drops to his elbows. "Yeah?"

"Yeah. I saw pictures of it."

"Oh? Do you have someone waiting for you up there?"

"She's not waiting for me," you say, before you can stop yourself. And then, with this out in the open, you see no reason to hold on to the rest any longer. "She has a boyfriend. Not that it's any of your business."

His head rears back in shock. "Did she tell you?"

"I've always known."

"So she's got her main boyfriend and then you on the side." He brings up a hand and with it makes a series of motions, indicating the boyfriend in a more central location and you on the periphery. Then he waves his hand around willy-nilly. "And you can fuck whoever?"

"Basically." That isn't it exactly, but basically.

"So you're going to tell her about me?"

"There isn't much to tell."

He glances at you—just a glance. You shrug, and he sighs.

You can tell this hurts him. You nudge his arm. It's supposed to be playful, but at the last second, you try to pass it off like you've lost your balance momentarily. He takes on that baffled look again. The cold nips at your chin and makes you think you might be sad, but that's not quite it. You look at Eli like you've only just understood why you brought him here. You say, "Do you want to fuck me?"

There's a moment's hesitation, in which he realizes that this has never been on the table—but now, suddenly, it just might be, if he plays it right. He tries to study your face, but you're not looking at him. You're breathing the cold, dark air. He says, "Yes." Then he adds: "We could do it in the back of the truck. It'd be warmer."

Quickly he understands that this wasn't the right thing to say, that there was never a right thing. You ask if you can just sit here awhile, and all he does is nod.

It grows quiet.

At last, he stands, swearing at his aching body. Somebody had to break that silence, and it was always going to be him. "I'm so out of shape," he says. "I'm like an old man. Jesus." And he offers you a hand to help you up.

"You never should've stopped running," you say without thinking.

He sighs but says nothing. You hope he doesn't think you feel sorry for him.

But he seems to know how he feels, and that's what matters. He doesn't try to explain his life or his decisions to you; he doesn't demand an apology, though you have to admit you've treated him dismissively, disdainfully. You let him lead you to the truck. He walks a couple steps ahead, all the while folding the blanket, stretching his arms out wide to do it. You think, This is it. This is the moment. All at once you think you've held this man in your hands, and you've already fallen in love with someone older—and meaner—and that's that. You'll fly back to Ithaca in just a few weeks. You'll get in late. You'll text her, and she'll be at the library, like always, and you'll go to her, like always. You'll never be able to forget it. Those stacks. The air, thick with dust and paper. The big knit of her scarf, your hat discarded, her fingers creeping up your spine like a chill or a silverfish. You're fully clothed and that is often the case. It's like this: her face pushed inside your jacket, a hand between your legs, light reflecting over and again in the window until there is no night, only this thing lost to history, this thing lost even as it's happening.

I'm Unarmed

Andie was my only friend in Prospect, Oregon. It was a small town with four churches and six hundred residents in just a few square miles. When my mother and I arrived, it was six o'clock in the morning, and my uncle wasn't expecting us. He hadn't seen my mother in years—not since he got wasted at her wedding and told her marrying my father was a mistake—but he wasn't surprised to hear that she'd left him and that now we had nowhere else to go. My uncle agreed to help us out until we got back on our feet. He ordered my cousin to make the bottom bunk, because we'd have to share a bedroom. I knew then that I was in trouble: his room was small, cold, and male. There was no light, no moon. I wouldn't be able to see his hand if he reached for me, but for the first week there was no threat of that. He was too scared to try anything, always pausing at the slightest sound. In his moments of ecstasy I wanted to shout, "Your mother hates you! All the way from Heaven."

My only respite from this was Andie. On the first day of school, we ran into each other in the halls, and though I was new in town and my cousin gave her a look that could've cut a lemon, she found me after our last class and asked if I wanted to hang out. I'd just spent the day avoiding my cousin's friends, who had taken to pinching their noses whenever they passed and saying P.U. as if they could smell the street on me, so naturally I hesitated, glancing all around in case it was a trap. When I confirmed that no one was watching us, I leaned in close and said, "What do you know about fortifications?"

We circled back to Andie's for provisions, double-checking to make sure her father's dark green truck wasn't in the drive. She'd promised sodas, chips, and fruit, and if not for her mother, I think she would've taken the whole fridge. When she ran out of the house, she was carrying a BB gun and her backpack. A voice said, "Andrea, when will you be back? I'd like to know where you're going." But Andie just kept running. She didn't stop until she turned the corner and had to double back. "That's my mother," she panted, as she fell in beside me. Her cheeks were flushed, and she slung the gun over her shoulders like a yoke. "I'll get the third degree when I get back."

I shrugged. We both did. "Why do you have that gun?"

"Oh this? It just shoots BBs." Her father had given it to her for Christmas, and she'd been practicing ever since, getting good with it. "I'm practically the best shot in this county," she said, shrugging like it was nothing. On our afternoons out, Andie always brought her BB gun with her. She'd shoot at snakes, rabbits, once or twice into the river. Prospect was nestled deep inside a national forest, so there was always some form of game to hunt. I saw men shoot birds out of the sky, saw deer stumble wounded into traffic and turtles cut open at their soft seams, but I never hurt an animal, not like that.

Andie and I excavated every inch of those woods, turned over rotting logs to find insects, threw rocks at every hornet's nest and took off running, every girl for herself. I began to feel as if I were home only when I was in the wild, gunshots echoing through the eaves, Andie sticking me with her problems, all those petty grievances that came and went while we climbed trees. I spoke infrequently and without much heart, occasionally giving Andie advice for love like: "Don't. Just don't." I never told her about my cousin. He had begun guiding my hand, and it would be spring before he began to guide my mouth as well. He never mentioned Andie, never said a word to or about her, but at night, when he pinned my arms down and demanded that I look at him, I could tell that he hated her, that he was punishing me for talking to her, for allowing her to walk me to and from class. I understood his jealousy. It was how I knew that Andie wanted me, too.

*   *   *

We settled into a rhythm. Andie had softball practice every other day, and we would meet out by the bleachers to head to the park. Our school team was the Lady Cougars. While they practiced, I sat in the grass near third base, catching foul balls with the glove Andie let me borrow. I have to say, they weren't very good, the Lady Cougars. They could catch the ball, and they could throw, but Lord knows they couldn't hit. Nearly every pitch wound up being a grounder, a pop. Once, Andie sliced the ball and smacked a girl on the thigh. Then, on an otherwise ordinary day, Andie cracked a clean, long drive across the ballpark, and I realized: she wanted me to join the team. Her coach even called the house to suggest it.

My uncle was home that day. He stood in the kitchen making a fresh pot of coffee, while my mother sat through a long lecture about the benefits of team sports: the character building, the exercise. When it was over, he leaned back against the counter and said, "That Silvan girl's a bad influence." There had been rumors about us. All of them circumstantial. When I said it was innocent—we were just friends—he shook his head. He said, "You can find better friends," as if it were obvious. "This town is full of good, hardworking people and nice, God-fearing children who would *help* you if you *let* them. I don't know why you're

100

afraid to talk to people." He started bending over to wipe up a coffee spill and scowled horribly when my mother told him to give me a break.

It isn't easy going to a new school. "She just needs some time to adjust."

"She's had time, and she's wasted it. She can barely say hi to me."

My mother threw up her hands. "It's just a softball team. She doesn't have to join."

"Well." He squeezed the sponge with an air of finality, taking the time to rinse it clean.

My mother told him she wouldn't force me to do anything I didn't want to do, but it didn't matter. Their conversation was already over. He went down to Medford, and my mother put on her uniform, pulling her hair back in a ponytail as she told me she was going to deep clean the pizza ovens that day. "I'm so *excited*."

When my mother was gone, I headed straight to Andie's, where the daphne was in bloom and the bumblebees were humming. We spent the day at our spot: an old, abandoned shack with a rusted pickup in front, rotten boards inside, and what used to be a tire swing before the animals chewed through the rope. Some days, after a particularly hard practice, we'd sit with our backs to the door, chucking pebbles into the tire. She'd bring sandwiches, pilfered beer. It was nice. "My uncle doesn't want me to see you anymore," I said.

Andie paused, trying to be brave. "What did he say about me?"

I dug my face into her shirt, telling her they were fighting, my mother and him. There had been several fights—all of them secret and terse, conducted when they thought my back was turned, though I always heard. "I don't know what he's going to do."

She stroked my hand hopefully. "What do you want?"

"I want my friend," I cried, but even then I knew this wasn't what Andie wanted to hear. When she handed me a beer, later, I saw the hurt in her face and the care she took in hiding it. "It just makes me so mad. It's like he thinks he owns me."

Her solution was to say the hell with him. "Here," she said, standing up and offering me a hand. "I'm going to teach you how to shoot this gun." Not the BB gun, but a real pistol—a hand-me-down her uncle had given her when he saw how good her aim was getting. She lined up all the empty bottles she could find on the hood of the pickup, then settled in behind me, steering the gun into my hands. "Spread your legs, or the recoil will knock you back." That made Andie taller than me, giving her space to bend her knees between my thighs. I could feel her legs under mine, feel her chin resting on my shoulder, her hands, the way they let go just as I was about to pull the trigger. I missed, but I did it on my own, shooting again and again until finally I hit one bottle.

I walked over to survey the damage. My misses had been wide misses, bullets ricocheting into the woods, but my hit had been solid, sure; the bullet broke the neck off the bottle, shattering it into long, jagged pieces I pinched between my fingers, wondering if they'd cut. Andie took the gun away, pleased with my performance, and lay back on the ground, sighing blissfully. I saw no reason not to join her then. It was late afternoon, light pouring through the trees. My sweatshirt, a gift from Andie, glowed crimson in the sun, its letters spelling DePaul, where her mother went to college. Andie was rubbing a stone with her fingers—a flat, smooth stone like the kind she might skip. "I snuck down to the Peninsula last night," she said.

I turned my head to the side, but she was staring at her hands, their slow, steady motion.

"I thought I might wake you," she said, then pressed the stone to her lips and told me she ran into the Hayward boy. Just him. None of his friends. "We kissed." There was a quiet then, like she was trying to tell me something else. After a long moment, she turned on her side, her face thin and serious. "Have you ever kissed a boy?"

"Yes."

"What was it like?"

I couldn't answer. I stared at the leaves falling around us. At how their crinkled points got lost in the strands of her hair. There was dirt on her cheek, a smear just below the bone, so I wiped it away with my thumb. This moved her, and she leaned in, fitting her lips to mine, asking nothing of me except that I understand. I closed my eyes in order to ground myself, feeling a light blow through me, feeling blood rush to my wrist and to my ears, where Andie put her hands in my hair and stroked. I let her kiss me for a long time.

When she broke away, I said, "You're a liar."

I sat up, hissing at the pebble in my back, then kicked at a beetle moseying across a mossed-over tire. She didn't restrain me. When I heard her breathing behind me, I stood. I knew I wasn't going back to my uncle's—I knew that—but I kept walking in that direction, and when I came to the roots of a tree I didn't know what to do, so I started to climb. Andie followed after a time, settling farther down on the opposite side. She shut her eyes, leaning her head against the trunk. "Are you going to be mad at me forever?"

"I'm not mad," I said, realizing for the first time that I never had been. "I just don't know where to go from here."

We took turns riding her bike to school. One pedaling, the other walking, neither setting a pace. Andie often had to double back for me. These mornings with the bike I loved unequivocally. The start of a day was a fresh thing: rising early before my cousin, eating cereal in my socks, and waiting for my only friend to come collect me. Those were the days I let Andie kiss me, her hand on my cheek, her fingers cold as dawn; then we'd ride, bike out of the way to arrive late to school or else early enough to smoke a cigarette. She was gentle with me. She didn't make me do anything I didn't want to, and in the afternoons she entertained me, read me books she liked, and watched over me while I napped. She'd seen me wince getting in and out of chairs at school, and she knew what that meant. I didn't tell her, but she knew. My cousin had stopped holding back.

At night, I held the thought of Andie's love in my mind. I knew it wouldn't protect me. I knew when my cousin reached for me that love was small and puny and that if I was to survive it would have to become something efficient, like hatred. He had no idea who I was: the rage I felt for him every minute, every hour. He thought I was weak, just a weak little girl, and when he came looking for me after lunch one day he expected me to be alone. He took pleasure in saying the principal was looking for me. "It has something to do with your grandma dying."

I don't remember what I said. It might've just been no, *no*, as in, "I don't want to hear it." Andie took one look at me then and jumped in, asking him, "Are you sure you aren't just reliving your mom's death? I remember how you cried like a little bitch." But I knew it was the truth from the way he stared at me and didn't even flinch at the mention of his mother. Maybe it was the look in his eye, like the weight of his gaze the morning after he first made me swallow, or maybe it was Andie's anger coursing through me—all the rage of her love—that made me hit him.

He was so accustomed to complacency that my attack caught him off guard. It was easy to floor him, incapacitate him with a few hard kicks to the groin. I could hear Andie back up against the locker, hear my cousin's nose break when I brought my geometry book down—again, again. Then again, maybe it was the thought of my grandmother dying alone, without anyone she loved or even anyone she hated as much as my father around to care for her body in the last of its indignities. I later learned that it was a heart attack, that one of my aunts had been by her side, and that it had happened months before, the week after our arrival in Oregon. My mother and I hadn't been informed because no one knew before then how to reach us. That my cousin was the one to tell me this was the final insult, and he paid for it dearly: he had to get dentures for the gaps I left in his smile, and he would limp for life after what I did to his leg.

It wasn't Andie who stopped me, but the vocational education teacher. There were a few students hovering in the hall, watching. I stilled the moment hands gripped at my sleeves, but even this did not satisfy the apprehension of the other teachers, some of whom held their hands over their mouths in shock, looking around as if my rage had broken like a kneecap and scattered its bones in the plaster. I looked around with them, expecting to see cracks.

*   *   *

My mother and I went back to living in the car. Instead of pressing charges, my uncle, the police, and the school tried to cover it up, pretend nothing happened. It was easier for our neighbors to believe Prospect was a nice town when they didn't have to say, "Oh, those kids went to jail," in hushed voices. Sometimes, I'd see my uncle around, and he would pause and, not in an unkind manner, try to rearrange his world into one where my cousin was good and I was just an ungrateful child he could scowl at and forget—but of course we never talked. In the afternoons, I met up with Andie, who started stealing things for me, bringing me milk and cookies and books she'd pinched from the library. She kept suggesting we run away. "We could go to Portland or Seattle—anywhere you want. We have the gun," she said, cradling it in her hand as if we could shoot our way down the coast. She was so sweet, I thought—so sweet and naïve, her face like that of someone trying to look tough.

"You're not cut out for that kind of life," I told her, because it was true.

"Why would you say that? I'm trying to protect you."

"What do you think I'm doing?"

She shook her head. "I can't believe you." Her mouth was open, and there was something deep inside her about to break, but rather than let me see it, she walked away. I didn't stop her. It was quiet then: no more talk about my cousin, no more threats that she was going to kill him, just silence and the fast, fumbling sound of a pair of football players hiking to the river. They weren't interested in me and there was no reason for me to be worried, but I still held on to the gun, which Andie had left for me in what she must've considered a profound gesture of love. I kept thinking maybe Andie would double back, tell me she was sorry, but when she didn't come to me I didn't go to her.

My mother was asleep when I returned. Her uniform was damp with sweat, and her shoes had tracked dirt onto the seat, probably without her noticing. I laid my head on her chest, and she roused just long enough to tell me my cousin had come into the diner that day for pizza; he'd asked how I was with such a look on his face, she threw his water at him, ice and all.

"Did they fire you?"

"It's just as well. We should leave before anyone else gets hurt." Even then, I wondered if it was me, if I was the dangerous one, or if she was just referring to the lengths she would go to in order to protect me. Sometimes, she wrapped me in her arms and held me tight until I couldn't breathe, because she was afraid of what would happen if she let go. When she fell asleep again, I went to Andie's.

By then, the temperature had dropped, and I was shivering in the grass as I began plotting my ascent to Andie's window. Her father had banned me from the house, so I had to be quiet scaling the tree. I settled on a low branch, peering hard through the window to where she sat, face obscured, bending over her book report. I'm still surprised she let me in. Her desk light was on, and anyone might've seen us, but I was so desperate for her kiss that I'd barely gotten my footing before I started pulling her to me and down.

"I'm still mad at you," she gasped, fighting a smile.

There was a half bath attached to her room, so we started there. I had the gun tucked into my pants, in the hem of my jeans, where its butt pressed into my belly button. The metal was still warm when she touched it hesitantly and with great restraint. She took the time to open the clip, breathing, "Good," when she counted the bullets. I stepped in the shower and started washing my hair. Andie had never seen me naked before, and she was hesitant to touch me. Once I was clean, she threw on some clothes to tell her parents she was going to bed. It was early, just eight thirty, and fog was creeping up, pressing against her window like a loving hand. Maybe, if the light was just so, I would wake to tell her I might never see her again, but for the moment I didn't even think to say that I was leaving. In the dark, I slid into bed, and I waited.

She returned with a cookie on a little white plate. "I thought you might get hungry."

I gestured to her bedside table, where she set the plate down and soon forgot it; the sheets had fallen away from my chest. I reached out to unzip her jeans, pulling them off to find she was naked underneath. Andie was a careful lover, and she made me come in her mouth so slowly and quietly, it felt like gliding, like slipping right off my axis and into the sun.

I woke as the sky was beginning to brighten. I ate the cookie she'd brought me, then went around the room, trying to capture the details that reminded me of her: the scent of her shirt, the picture of her asleep, the books she kept in her pocket, their supple covers and broken spines. I lifted the gun, considering its heft, but it only reminded me of my cousin and of the thought that she might kill him, so I left it in the drawer where it belonged. I brushed my hair, preparing to leave, but then I got the idea of cutting it short, like Andie's. I didn't really know what I was doing, so I just started cutting. The hair I cut off, I left on the floor, where Andie would find it and know that I was never coming back.

SAFEKEEPING

When it was first arranged, her lover said she would be safe: the apartment was designed just like a vault. No matter what happened, the doors would lock, the water would run, and the overhead lights would continue to shine in their metallic, cage-like sconces; the whole world could descend into nuclear winter, and the apartment would remain a comfortable 72°F (except for the cold spot in the bathroom and the caul of heat around the oven whenever she made her dinners). There was a lifetime supply of dehydrated food in the cupboards and an intercom should she need to request anything, though where the intercom led and who it was connected to, she did not know. Once or twice, she tried pressing the button and shouting, "Hello. Hello?" But there was no answer. There was nothing she needed, anyway. Everything had been provided for, except her loneliness.

*

They had staged it like a kidnapping—a broken window, signs of a struggle. Her lover even drew a blood sample to plant her DNA on the carpet, where investigators would see it and presume her kidnapper had been violent. Partial footprints (men's size nine Georgia Boots with thick, commando lugged soles) made it look like the kidnapper had approached through the garden and lain in wait until she returned from her daily office hours on campus. That he waited in her bedroom, pawing through her closet and underwear drawer (both of which were left open), was meant to mislead investigators, make them believe that the suspect was some kind of sexual predator—a deviant—whose subterranean desires made him statistically unlikely to be found even if investigators had limitless time and resources—which they did not. Manpower was scarce, and without any real leads there was little detectives could do. Their investigation stalled out quickly. Memorials were held. Friends and family paid their respects. Many had a hard time accepting the official story of her disappearance, and none of them learned the truth. Her lover stayed behind to make sure of that.

*

Prior to going underground, her lover provided her with a packet of fake identities: falsified birth certificates, identification cards, passports, records of immunization, diplomas. Given that the safe house was located one hundred meters underground, it was very unlikely that anyone would ever find her, and, in the event that they did, she was instructed never to divulge her birth name. Not even if the person (or persons) who located her claimed to work with her lover at Hardwater, the private military contractor that employed her lover as a cybersecurity specialist. In fact, her lover had personally designed, tested, and built all the automated systems in this very bunker, which was Hardwater's signature product. Hundreds of these safe houses had been built for high-paying customers (businessmen, diplomats, military leaders) in anticipation of the war. Her lover had hidden this location from Hardwater by hacking into their systems and masking her virtual communications with the construction team, which she had handpicked from the company's pool of civilian laborers. To them, this project was just one of many and there was no reason to believe otherwise or to suspect that the man funding it was just a fiction; to Hardwater, it didn't exist, just as she herself didn't exist.

*

Her lover insisted she have no contact with the outside world. To maintain their ruse that she was missing, presumed dead, her parents could never know she was alive. She could never call their house on Christmas morning or ask them out to dinner. When their birthdays came, on June 4 and August 9, she could not climb the staircase and leave the safe house to see them. At least, not if she wanted to come back. That was why she stayed: the thought that her lover might return and build a life with her there in the comforts of their own home. It could be welcoming, in a strange, programmable way. All the windows were artificial, their screens designed to alter with each season, so in the spring there were lilacs and in the fall, colors. Still, on those mornings when she knew it was winter, she longed for nothing more than a glass of good mulled wine and some blankets she could wrap around her shoulders as she snuggled closer to a fire. It seemed her lover had thought of everything, except for the smell of leaves burning in a barrel and the taste of snow crabs dipped in butter. There was no recourse for nostalgia or desire.

*.

On-screen, icicles clung to telephone wires and streets previously dotted with trash cans and recycling bins were painted white, each pixel representing a thousand individual snowflakes in a picture only she could see. This street, that snowplow, those little kids running around the corner—none of it was real. It had all been simulated. If she put her hand on a window, it would not feel cold, though frost seemed to be choking the glass, closing in around it like a hand on a throat. Instead, the screen would ripple a bit, distorting the picture, as a wave of pixels colored the snow. It could be purple, she knew, or pink or an odd shade of orange, like a finger held up to a flashlight. Someone had animated it. Chosen a wholesome little street in a quiet little town where children could play outside without fear of being kidnapped or run over. She had watched the windows long enough to know that there was some continuity: families moved in and out, women got pregnant, trucks broke down, kids fell off their bikes one morning, then reappeared wearing Band-Aids the next. Entire storylines flared up and died while she sat in her living room, counting the hours.

*

Sometimes, she felt stifled by her safety. Following a set routine helped. Mornings were for self-improvement: a high-protein breakfast, followed by moderate exercise, one half hour of language practice, an hour of reading, painting, a shower, and some light gardening. Her apartment (as she liked to call it) came equipped with a small hothouse, where she grew tomatoes and zucchini and pruned her basil plants before they flowered. Life was simpler. She no longer worried about how much nitrogen oxide had been released into the atmosphere or whether the earthworm population would rebound after the war. In this apartment, she was no longer a respected scientist, and it did not matter that in graduate school she was among the first people to witness almendro trees shrinking into their roots (the bat population was also shrinking—and, with it, the

almendro's primary source of guano). Following gradua-
tion, she was offered a research position and awarded a
grant to support her experiments in terraforming. Earth
needed recalibration. More oxygen in its atmosphere, less
carbon in its oceans. A commitment to maintaining its
biodiversity before its entire ecosystem collapsed. In her
lab at the university, she genetically modified plants to
produce fourteen to sixteen times the amount of oxygen
per day. If given the time and resources, she might have
been able increase that tenfold. But it was too late. War
loomed on the horizon. Hardwater had known ahead of
time when it would begin. But had it happened? Had Earth
descended into chaos? It was impossible to say.

*

Her lover had been gone over six months when she decided she couldn't take it anymore. She had to get out.
Her apartment was connected to the surface by way of a
tall, circular staircase. Its walls were reinforced with steel
to prevent collapse, and the door (a new magnesium alloy
as light as aluminum and as strong as titanium) required
a ten-digit passcode, a handprint, and a retinal scan. Once
opened, the door led directly to a tunnel to the surface.
She had been blindfolded when she first arrived and didn't
know where she would emerge. Her lover had supplied
her with a parka, mittens, snowshoes, and pants made
from water-resistant, military-grade fabric. Outside, the

cold wind was blistering and shrill. With her knit scarf wrapped around her mouth, she trudged toward the ruins of a small town. The mailboxes she passed on the way were riddled with bullet holes; shards of broken glass glinted in the mounds of snow outside the abandoned storefronts. Overhead, helicopters chopped the air up. They belonged to the military, which appeared to occupy this territory. What had become of the world, she wondered. Was the war still raging? Perhaps. She worried that some of the soldiers had seen her. One helicopter circled back, dipped, then pulled away to rejoin its platoon. She didn't trust them to leave her in peace. She hurried back to the safe house, brushing away her boot prints as she traveled so the soldiers wouldn't be able to track her without dogs. It had been so stupid of her to leave. What if the apartment had been breached in her absence? What if her lover had returned, only to find her gone? Once safely inside, she reset the alarm and vowed never to leave again. There was nothing left for her on the surface, not anymore. Thinking of everything that had been lost, she crawled in bed and cried herself to sleep. She woke as stars began to appear in the windows. On the screens, in bright white pixels, a message shone: I'll be back tonight.

And so she waited.

*

It became a sort of ritual—laying her clothes out on the bed, putting the water in the kettle. It had taken her hours to get ready the first night. She spilled water on the floor and got a comb stuck in her hair as she scrambled to boil the halibut and rehydrate the wine; then, when the table was set, there was nothing more she could do except light the candles and eat the figs she had been saving for the occasion. There was a limited amount of everything, particularly fruit, but she wanted this dinner to be perfect and waited as long as she could before sinking her teeth into the fig's flesh; even then she felt guilty (the skin had gotten sticky, and the acids in the juice had eaten their way through the greens until the salad became mushy, the lettuce dark and slimy as the sea). Her sole comfort in these moments was the thought that she had grown all these vegetables herself, that the kale and the mustard greens and the ripe tomatoes had arisen from her own soil: clean, unadulterated soil, free of toxins and fed by the purest water possible, water that had been treated with ultraviolet light rather than disinfectants so its taste wouldn't be tainted by chemicals. It was thoughtful of her lover to make that change (all the other safe houses used a filtration system that made the water taste sterile). It was comforting to think that she was taken care of. Even after she accepted that her lover wasn't coming, there was still the dinner. There was still the wine and the fish and the lovely béchamel she had made with the rehydrated milk and the last of the Parmesan cheese. After all, she was wearing that dress—the one her lover bought her from France, with the sleeveless arms and naked back. It had a cowl neck, its folds accentuating the soft lines of her throat and the hard edge of the necklace wrapped so tight around her neck, by the end of the third course she felt like she was choking.

*

There were cracks in the ceiling. She might not have noticed them, except one morning she woke up yearning for a proper lab, with phosphorus and zinc and grad students wearing safety goggles, and to console herself she laid in bed reading old science journals about plant physiology and the epigenetic influence of oxygen deprivation on the life cycle of bean plants. Then she laid back on a pillow, and there they were: hairline cracks, like a root system in the ceiling. For a moment, she thought she could see them growing. It was difficult to say how long they'd been there. If she had to guess, she would say that it had been months. The cracks extended the length of the ceiling and protruded slightly in the center, as if taking on water; but the paint was very dry to the touch, and she knew (because her lover had told her) that behind it there was plaster, then foam, then steel, a thick layer of it designed to withstand any blast. If the ceiling were to collapse, it would mean the tectonic plates were shifting, the earth itself packing and unpacking as if under the pressure of an eternal grave digger whose shovel was seeking the edges of her home, hoping to undermine it (and she did worry that something had come loose along the way—the air ducts pried from their hinges, the stairway drifting farther from the door). If she had but been left the proper tools, she could have investigated the matter, attempted some sort of do-it-yourself fix; but her lover had insisted she have only the most basic equipment and had all but outlawed any science experiment or building project. The apartment's systems were very delicate and should not be tampered with, her lover had said. But what would she do if they failed?

*

In the fall, when the artificial windows gleamed with the light of a billion changing leaves, a tiny glitch in the mainframe resulted in the images being projected inward, like holograms. She could see the lines where the computer mapped the images, connecting dots to form three-dimensional figures, like that of a cat or a tree. She saw a young girl cycling through the kitchen, her pale hair and knitted scarf streaming behind her, as in a breeze. It happened that her couch was positioned under a maple tree, and when she curled up under its branches with a cup of tea, its leaves began falling all around her, their luminous, fiery ribs passing quietly through her chest. It lasted three hours—maybe four—until a second glitch, no doubt precipitated by the first, resulted in this faint illusion flickering in and out of sight. For days after, she saw things in the corner of her eye: the laces of a football sailing through the air, the tail of a squirrel twitching fretfully as it counted its nuts. And once, in bed after drinking a package of white wine, she awoke when a pair of headlights burst to life inside her dresser. She had to shield her eyes to see the ghostly outline of a truck emerging through the wall. Someone killed the engine. There was a man sitting at the wheel, fingers lifting the pale ghost of a cigarette as he nodded at an accomplice. There was an exchange of words and a hard crack like a skull hitting the floor, and then the apparition disappeared, never to return.

*

Her nightmares were waking her up two, three times a night. In one, she was locked inside an old building where the only method of escape was to descend a rusty ladder and crawl through the heating ducts to reach sewers. In another, she was gliding through the halls of an enormous palace, admiring the gilded chairs and inlaid mirrors. Suddenly, she sensed she wasn't alone. She ducked into a dressing room, where she shut herself inside an antique wardrobe, thinking that she was in danger; even in the midst of perfect luxury, this was always what she thought. Her dreams had taken on a sinister quality, both bizarre and claustrophobic, as if her subconscious mind were attempting to warn her of something.

And then one night her lover visited her in her dreams.

*

It was impossible to say whether it did or did not happen. Thinking back on it, she remembered dreaming of a gravel road, the crunch of rocks under her shoes as she walked through the parking lot of a dive bar. Inside, she met a man sorting through his dirty laundry.

He said, "You shouldn't be here." This was true.

She responded, "My girlfriend's going to be here soon." He had no response to this, other than to sort his laundry.

Suddenly, the scene changed. She found herself standing in the corner of a small, triangular room in a stranger's house. She was at a party. She said, "Someone's here," to the sound of knocking at the door, and then there was the feeling of a hand stroking her hair and rolling her over in bed. At the exact moment when bikers crashed through the window and destroyed her terrariums, she tilted her head back, her vision going black as she rose into a slow, inevitable kiss. Her hands had been tucked under the covers but soon drifted up to rest on her lover's cheeks. When she kissed harder, her lover's tongue caught the corner of her mouth. The next thing she knew, the kiss was over and her lover had pulled back. She asked, "Why did you stop?" thickly, slowly, as if trying to draw the words from the air and arrange them on her tongue.

Her lover materialized in front of her, her lips curving into a wan, beneficent smile. "I'm sorry I've been away so long," she cried, her face cracking, then falling like the cliff of a giant iceberg upending itself in the dark. When her lover started to babble about Hardwater and the assassins they sent after her, she began the gentle process of making her quiet: small shushing noises, hands on her cheeks, the words "come here" followed by a kiss or an attempt at one. Her lips met nothing, only air. Thinking about it, after, it occurred to her that she might've pulled too hard and that this was why her lover abruptly pushed her away. Looking at her hand, she found it empty, the heel of her palm warm and soft where her lover's cheek had been. It took a long time to comprehend this. "Where did you go?"

"I'm right here."

With great effort, she lifted her gaze from her palm to see her lover standing by the bed. "You're here," she breathed. "Are you real? Am I dreaming?" A tremor of betrayal passed over her lover's face, but in its wake there was only sorrow and hesitation as to how to proceed. Her lover knelt, allowing a hand to slide under her shirt. What happened next, she did not know. She woke the next morning with her head propped on the staircase, her hand grazing the locked magnesium door. In her dream, she hadn't been able to remember their pass code, so she had slept there, ruined and spent, believing that if she closed her eyes the dream world and the real world would unravel and she would know. The war was over. They had lost.

*

In the days and weeks after it happened, she kept turning the dream over in her mind, replaying it as if it were a cherished film written and directed with her edification in mind (see how much she loves you, this film seems to say; see when your skin starts to burn how her hand smooths away the sweat as if you have a fever). One evening, the apartment's system projected the image of her lover onto a chair in the dining room. She forgot herself so thoroughly that she sat and spoke to it for a full half hour before she realized it couldn't respond (it didn't know how). Night after night, her lover appeared in bed, and she was so grateful for this small kindness that she crawled inside the projection's ghostly outline and slept there, heart to heart. She understood now that she would die in this safe house. If not of old age, then of the ceiling caving in or the pipes bursting or a gas leak or some other fault of technology or mechanics. This apartment would keep her alive for as long as it could. Then, when her time came, it would bury her, sealing her forever in a place where the world could not reach her, where she was safe from bombs and pestilence and distrust, free to die in her own time and on her own terms. And when that happens she will know that she was loved.

.

The Twilight Hotel

Our anniversary is coming up. Seven years this November. We like to count from our first date rather than our wedding day, because when I proposed, gay marriage wasn't yet legal in New York State. Aimee and I were one of the first lesbian couples to get married at city hall in July of 2011. Thanks to the reporters present that morning, some of our wedding photos are still floating around online. If you happen to find a picture of us, I'm the one in the white tuxedo beaming up at Aimee while she throws the bouquet at one of the photographers. It's a gentle toss—one she warned him about and prepared him for. Her face is bright with happiness as she lets go, releasing the flowers like a magician freeing a dove. I haven't seen that expression in a long time.

About a year ago, Aimee and I started talking about having children. "I just feel like we put it off for all the wrong reasons," she said, citing our long wait to marry and our inability to get pregnant on our own. It was time, we decided. We consulted a doctor and a lawyer, readied the papers we would need so I could adopt our child after it was born. Aimee wanted to carry it to term. She was twenty-eight then, two years younger than I was, and in better shape. I had been a smoker in my youth, and my family had a history of heart disease. Aimee's genes were perfect, as were the sperm donor's. His file said he graduated summa cum laude and played rugby in his spare time, but that mattered less than the fact that he looked like me: brown hair, brown eyes, a round face that would have been plain if not for the curve of his cheekbones and the shapeliness of his mouth. Aimee called them that: shapely. His sperm arrived in an insulated container so we could handle the insemination ourselves, at home, where Aimee would be comfortable. We lit candles, played some relaxing music. Somehow, it never occurred to us to be afraid of a miscarriage.

It has been ten weeks. She doesn't talk about it.

Our life has continued much as it did before, with the pleasant weeks of June giving way to a predictably hot and stifling August. Heat always exacerbates Aimee's insomnia. For a month now she has been slipping out of bed in the middle of the night and sitting in the darkened living room, listening to jazz radio at such a low volume that I can barely hear it. Sometimes, when I find her there at one or two in the morning, she turns to me with an expression I can't bear to see, because I know she's trying to find the right words for something unspeakable.

Desperate to cheer her up, I surprised her with tickets to the Village Vanguard last night.

"Think of it as an early anniversary present."

Aimee pulled her face into something like a smile.

"Or we could just stay in," I said. "Order Thai food." Quickly, I rattled off half a dozen movies in our queue, knowing, all the while, that I was too late. Aimee had already clicked into autopilot. I watched, disappointed, as she went through the motions of getting ready.

"We can take our time. Our dinner reservations aren't until seven thirty."

She nodded. She'd just finished applying lipstick and was staring miserably at her mouth.

I hailed the taxi for us.

Our waiter was a young white man with pierced ears and an asymmetrical haircut. He smiled unpleasantly when Aimee said, "I'd like a bottle of Riesling, please," before we even properly sat down.

Once he left, I said, "Aimee."

"What? I'm pretty happy with the decision."

"There's a one-drink minimum at the Vanguard. You're not going to make it."

At this she merely raised her eyebrows and took a sip of water.

I waited until her second glass of wine to ask, "Did something happen at work?"

"Did something happen," Aimee repeated ruefully. Then it was just a matter of sitting there and trying not to interrupt as she told me how one of her coworkers had just returned from maternity leave and was so excited about the baby and the pictures. She asked Aimee, "So when are you due?" And then she immediately got this look on her face, because she realized it had been four months already and Aimee wasn't showing.

"She just caught me off guard—I thought I was done with all that." The having to tell people, she meant, and seeing the pity in their faces. We'd made the mistake of telling everyone we got pregnant—everyone, including our bosses and coworkers. But, unlike pregnancy, a miscarriage is a private thing, and in its immediate aftermath it never occurred to us that there would be people we left behind, people we didn't see that often, who would go on with their lives, assuming that it was okay, that we were five weeks, ten weeks, sixteen weeks pregnant. *Smile! You're having a baby!* That was our story.

She'd given up on dinner by then. Instead of eating, she flaked the sole apart, easing the tines of her fork between the individual layers of flesh, separating them. Soon the fish was like a chain of uninhabited islands in a shimmering, translucent sea. I stopped trying to talk to her and instead ate in silence, sitting vigil as one hoped-for narrative ended and another more painful one began. Once or twice, her head dipped dramatically, and I feared she would slip out of consciousness; but she always came back.

The waiter knew nothing of our troubles. He checked on us toward the end of the meal and asked if Aimee would like another bottle of wine, and because he said this in an ugly way, seeing the glass in her hand and the dull hollow of the bottle nearly spent, she hissed at him that the fish was dry. He scurried into the kitchen and returned with apologies from the chef and the house's dessert special: a bourbon caramel custard with almond shortbread and lavender whipped cream. He also brought a pair of candles wrapped in glass so sinuous and thick that when the wax melted it made the light float over the table. Our wineglasses shimmered. Our unused cutlery collapsed into puddles, and outside the orange line of the sunset bled down behind the city, then disappeared.

I wondered aloud where the evening had gone.

Idly, I asked myself, "What if there were a place where the sun was always setting?"

Aimee managed to hear this. "What do you mean, *always*?"

"Always. That it would just keep setting. It'd never reach the horizon."

"That's impossible. It doesn't make *sense*," she said, her hand flopping severely in her lap.

I wished then that I'd never taken her to that restaurant, that we'd spent the night cuddling under a blanket, where I could stroke her face until she was close enough for me to whisper, "Let's pretend, okay? We're on an island in the sky."

Let that be the story: us waking up early, taking a plane, landing in an impossible place where the sun never stops setting. It would have to be flying. How else could the island keep up with Earth's rotation? How else can you figure it but as a fantastic dome supported by some impossible physics, costing some obscene amount of money, so that only the very rich can afford the trip? If it hadn't been my idea, Aimee and I wouldn't be able to swing it, but, since it was, we're treated like VIPs and given a luxury suite at the Twilight Hotel, where staff greets us in shiny shoes and designer sunglasses.

"It's best not to stare," the manager says when he sees me looking at the sunset, that red glare bleeding across the horizon. "It could disturb your circadian rhythms if you expose yourself before lunch."

I turn my back to the sun and gaze up at the hotel. One side of the hotel gleams under an armor of solar panels and sheet glass while the other side sulks in the shadows, lost to the sun forever. Everything here is pristine: the lush greenery, the stone carapaces, the various pools and fountains leading to the front doors. Inside, several sliding glass panels open and close to permit us entry into a cathedral of a lobby where four rectangular windows stretch from floor to ceiling, emitting an unearthly radiance (like television snow, but gold).

After dropping off our luggage we proceed to a banquet hall, where we eat poached eggs with smashed avocado and pancetta while old women in caftans berate their husbands, who ignore them. Early on, we notice an older man—a bachelor—with a deep orange tan that stands out against his crisp white collar. I ask Aimee, "Do you think he could be a spy? Maybe MI6?" She says he looks like old money and Cary Grant. We spend the rest of brunch giggling into our juice, because whenever the man needs attention he lifts one finger and cries out, "Waiter—oh, waiter!" with a peculiar tilt of his head, as if he's trying to detach it from his neck.

Brunch is followed by a trip to the spa, where I pour water onto the hot stones.

Aimee leans back against the wall and groans.

A devilish-looking man leans over, lifting his eyebrows. "You ladies having a hard time?"

"We're fine, thanks." I wave him off, flashing my wedding ring. This makes him grin.

"I understand. It's a lot to take in." He lifts his eyes to the ceiling, waving one hand lazily. Somehow, this man has snuck a scotch into the sauna, and what's left of the ice in his drink looks like a thin plastic chip when he swirls his glass.

He's about to take a sip when he suddenly lowers his drink. "Say, do you like tennis? How about we play tennis? They've got a nice court. Custom rackets. Showers . . ." His voice disappears under the rough burn of the scotch. He smacks his lips. "Of course, I intend to change my jacket before the Fish and Goose Soiree," he says. His eyebrows, with their wolfish peaks, remind me of Jack Nicholson's.

Instead of playing tennis, Aimee and I sit next to the pool, watching the high divers glisten like diamond-studded blades as their bodies cut through the air. Aimee is quiet and leans back in her pool chair, knees bent, hands resting neatly over her abdomen. It reminds me of the morning we lost the baby. Aimee sat alone in the bath-tub, hugging herself and waiting for the cramps to ease. I remember the water between her thighs turned pink, and her pajama top, which she hadn't bothered to take off, clung to her skin. Only nine hours before, I was resting my head on her stomach, thinking of the baby. I'd been hoping for a girl.

Against the advice of the hotel staff, I remove my sun-glasses and stare at the sunset. My heart starts to slow, and I fall asleep, thinking even as I dream that I'm still awake, that Aimee is still pregnant and nothing has gone wrong. It's less a belief than a state of being: I *am* having a baby. My wife *is* pregnant. In my dream, I know this for a fact. I walk around. I have these weird encounters. I sit on a beach, where a man suns his back, oblivious to the fact that sand crabs are burrowing into his skin—but I know. No matter what happens, I know that Aimee will join me on the beach soon and that when she stands in front of me her belly will be smooth and round, like a melon that isn't quite ripe.

I don't want to wake up, but when I do, Aimee says, "Happy hour just started."

I'm still sitting in the pool chair. Aimee isn't pregnant.

"Come on. We're going to be late."

Inside, the Fish and Goose Soiree has just started. It's being held in the Silver Lounge, a tasteful, monochromatic banquet hall with floor-to-ceiling mirrors that reflect the white leather armchairs and asymmetrical tables. It feels like the soiree is being held inside a large photograph in a home decor catalog. Waiters in white jackets and silver bow ties are positioned strategically throughout the banquet hall—not moving, just balancing their trays on one hand, like statues. At first glance, the trays appear to be laden with jewelry, but up close I can see that the pearls are in fact candies and the fresh strawberries are coated in edible gold and silver. Aimee bites into one skeptically, and the gold clings to her lips, making them glitter in the light.

We drift toward the bar, which is made of a frosted textured glass that glows from within, giving it the appearance of ice. Almost immediately, we find ourselves surrounded by a group of young independent filmmakers with a fondness for dark smoking jackets with bright red lapels. Instead of engaging, we cultivate a kind of drifting, listing attitude, so that, in bending our ears to one member of the group, we seem to dip in and out of every adjoining conversation and are thus spared from having to respond to one in particular. It is a relief when a bell rings, signaling that dinner is served. Aimee eats an entire goose and barely touches her wine. The elderly couples at our table have to shout to hear each other over the clattering of plates and utensils. After one man asks if she's single, Aimee turns to me and says, "Can we go?" I can't hear the words, but I can read her lips.

Halfway to the door, the presumptuous man from the sauna stops us. "Ladies," he says, stretching out his arms to prevent our passing. "I knew you'd come around." He grins at Aimee. "Is this for me?"

He means her dress: a shining silver ball gown paired with emerald earrings and an opal pendant. My gift to Aimee for our last anniversary.

"It's stunning. Come. Join us." He introduces us to his circle of friends: middle-aged men with more money than they know what to do with and beautiful girlfriends who are certainly not their wives, though I note a great many wedding rings. The Jack Nicholson look-alike has an arm wrapped around the waist of a young blond in kitten heels, who kisses his cheek sweetly. A well-groomed banker tilts his head in the middle of our conversation and asks of a

French filmmaker, "But don't you think he falls into the European trap of getting lost in the quotidian?"

Aimee finds this so absurd she has to stare into her drink to keep from laughing.

This happens again and again: one of us getting caught in a situation, so the other has to step in, make an excuse—a rescue—with apologies. I steer us onto a balcony, where one or two smokers nod quietly but show no real interest in us. I feel as if we've just come to the end of a long, grueling obstacle course. We're panting, shivering slightly in the cold shadow of the hotel. Aimee leans in close, as if to rest her head on my collarbone.

Very carefully, I ask if she's okay.

"I don't want to go back in there," she breathes. "Those people."

"I know."

"That guy earlier."

I shake my head. I don't even know where to begin.

Aimee presses a hand to her stomach. She ate too much. "I think I need to lie down."

Back in the room, I offer to help her undress, but she denies me and crawls into bed fully clothed.

While she sleeps I wander around the hotel. It's quiet now with all the guests at the soiree. Housekeeping takes advantage of the emptiness and does a round of cleaning. This, I think, is the highest reaching hotel in the world and the closest I'll ever get to the heavens. I pause to ask one of the housekeepers if it's possible for me to access the roof. She directs me toward the end of the hall, where I find a sign that says VIEWING GALLERY and points to what I might otherwise mistake for a dead end. The door is heavy, metal, and pulls shut with a scraping sound. For a moment, the hall is pitch black. Then—from below—a bright orange light blinks awake and draws a slow, thin line from my feet to the door at the end of the hall. It opens before I even reach it.

Inside, an automated voice says, "Welcome to the Twilight Hotel Viewing Gallery Two, floor fifty. We are currently flying over Ecuador. If you look to your left, you can see the peaks of the Andes Mountains, including Chimborazo, the tallest mountain in Ecuador, at twenty thousand five hundred and sixty-four feet. Local time is nine fifty-six p.m. Thank you for staying with us at the Twilight Hotel."

I look left, like the voice suggests, but I'm more interested in the sun than the mountains. Here, the sky looks shy and affectionate, glowing soft and pink, like it has a secret to share; but I can see anvil-shaped clouds in the corner of my eye and a streak of lightning that disappears like *that*. If I stand here until this time tomorrow, I will see Brazilian rain forests, African grasslands, island nations, and three separate oceans, all in the course of a day. We can go everywhere and nowhere and end up right where we started—with the same heartbreak, the same disappointment. I can feel thunder rumble in my heart like it's about to burst.

Aimee.

When I return, she's curled up on her side, sleeping. I can see her forehead tighten and relax as my weight settles on the mattress. I stretch out, mirroring her, and listen to her breathe. I can hear her trying to rouse, lifting herself from some deep layer of consciousness but never quite making it. All Aimee can manage is to stretch out her hand and press it in my own.

I wait a moment, then whisper, "Where are you?"

Her lips part. The words sweep out of her as in a dream: "Madagascar. A man getting hit by lightning. God."

I close my eyes. "It isn't real," I say. "Aimee. Come back to me, please."

She shakes her head, still half asleep. "We can't have a baby."

"I'm not asking for that."

She shakes her head again, this time with a whimper that says she's going to start crying. I try to hold her, to kiss her cheeks and stroke her hair, but she curls into herself, weeping as if I'm not even here. And that's the truth, isn't it? That we've grown so far apart I don't know how to reach her. It's like staring out at some distant river, knowing, without any real evidence to suggest it, that by the time you get there it'll be different, that the river will bend, the temperature rise, the current carry a dead brood of fish out to sea. I never thought we'd wind up here. She's the one. Aimee. Aimee, please. I know what comes next, and I'm not ready for it.

WEEKEND

When the first episode aired, Weston joked that if they made a second season he'd film an entire episode in the nude. It was an offhand remark born of the assumption that no one would be interested in avant-garde television, and if his costar and director hadn't spent the last nine years of their lives in studios and in off-off-Broadway productions, making art few people had heard of and even fewer had seen, they might've mistaken his tone for pessimism, questioned his devotion to the project, and wondered if he was really the right choice for this part. He had gotten lucky in that he did not have to wait to be understood and that they'd both laughed instantly, approvingly, chiming in with promises that sounded very much like threats: if he performed in the nude, Julia would begin writing songs for the show, and if Julia started singing, Ewan, the director, would be obliged to take them all to Maine, where his mother owned a small bed and breakfast, and where, in the midst of lobster traps and fishing boats, Julia's character,

141

Gwen, would hurl her engagement ring into the sea. This last bit ended up not coming true for the simple reason that Ewan had put a considerable down payment on the ring and decided that Gwen shouldn't call off the wedding, after all. Instead, the trip to Maine became a grand, romantic excursion for the main characters, one of many in the show's fifteen-year history, which Weston recalled with a fondness that reminded him of the myopia of youth.

He had never forgotten the joke, and when their funding was renewed for a second season he was the one to approach Ewan about the episode. It was agreed that Weston would decide the when and the how. If he did not feel comfortable with full-frontal nudity, Ewan would film it so that Weston would always be hidden behind a piece of furniture or a newspaper or even the curve of his own thigh. It was also agreed that he would not warn Julia ahead of time. When the day came, he would simply wake up, strip off his clothes, and pour himself a cup of coffee. She would then respond as she saw fit. It was standard practice for them to meet at Ewan's apartment on Friday nights and sleep together in his bed so when they woke up in the morning they would already be in character, rising not as Julia and Weston but as Josh and Gwen, a couple of twenty-something New Yorkers who were living together in a small charming apartment on the Lower East Side.

He had never known Julia to shy away from his touch or even wrinkle her nose at his morning breath, except where it was appropriate to Gwen's character, but they had never engaged in any intimate physical activity—on-screen or off. Everything they had done had been simulated, and he had never been fully nude in front of her, nor she in front of him. It did feel kind of comical: waking up right at the crack of dawn, peering over to her side of the bed, and then waiting to be sure she was truly asleep before taking off his shirt and underwear.

Ewan wasn't in the room then and had no knowledge of the decision Weston had made. He only got up when he heard Weston making coffee, and Weston had already been awake for an hour by then. He had slid his boxers off under the sheet and lain there long enough for his erection to swell, then ease, then leave him feeling jittery and in need of a bit of distance from Julia, whose sighs and murmurs had him staring helplessly at her lips. He took his time in the kitchen and strapped on a watch his character was fond of wearing. When he heard Ewan stirring, he checked the time: 7:15. It was September, and the days were already getting shorter.

Ewan sat down at the kitchen table and asked to be given a glass of water. He was, at that time, a man in his early thirties, unmarried, unusual, but with a camera and an editing program that assured him control over his artistic vision. He had managed to secure funds from a wealthy benefactor who had taken an interest in his films at an exhibition. His only instruction had been to make the art no one was interested in making. Hence, avant-garde television. The idea was to create a show about the weekend lives of a couple who worked in New York. There would be no plot, no scripts, no makeup, and no crew except Ewan himself and the man who mastered the audio. The focus of the show would be the emotional content, and there would be emphasis placed on the quotidian aspects of life (food, reading, conversation) that most television overlooked in favor of comedic one-liners and regular cliff-hangers. Because of this, Ewan imagined himself a great European director and entered his own kitchen in full awareness that he had made it into a set.

He took one look at Weston and said, "You haven't shaved."

Weston rubbed a hand over his stubble, but he knew that wasn't what Ewan meant.

"I don't think you should drink any coffee." It was decaf, but he could see it was only making Weston nervous, having something else to think about. He hadn't accepted his nudity yet, and he was still trying to cover himself with his character's routine: the watch, the coffee. He held the mug before him like a reminder that the day had just begun. Ewan said, "She's going to know you're stalling."

Weston's gaze flicked anxiously to the door. "Do you think she's listening?"

"You know how she is."

He did know. They had been working on this project for a little over a year, and though he felt he knew very little about Julia as a person (her quirks and eccentricities, to say nothing of her taste in men), he understood something of her process as a performer. He had seen her mouth fall open and the particulars of her identity float across her features as if unveiling that part of her that had been Gwen all along. It was less a rearranging of self than it was the arrival at an other that was as much a part of Julia as the ability to act or even to breathe. Whenever he saw Julia in character, it seemed to him that she had always been capable of this—this performance—as if she were, in some other life, a woman just like Gwen: a former barista who worked in sales and who over the course of the show would move into marketing, become an executive, and launch her own line of cable-knit infinity scarves, just for the fun of it. He knew, without having to articulate it, that the only reason she wasn't living that lifestyle was because she did not want it, just as she had no desire in this world or any world to see his penis. It would merely be there in front of her and she would have to find the place inside her that would respond; that was the part he had been dreading. He didn't want to see her gaze drift down his body and know that regardless of what he might see in her expression there was no real emotion in it. It was a ruse.

And so, he'd decided to be charming. When he was ready, he topped off his cup of coffee, gave Ewan the nod, and then waited until he'd set up the cameras before drumming his fingers on the door. He poked his upper body through the crack. "Gwen, are you awake?"

She stretched her arms out to the headboard, burying her face in the pillow.

"I was thinking of making breakfast."

Her head turned, her red hair obscuring her cheek. "I'm not hungry."

"Coffee?"

She shook her head. "I'll just have some of yours."

"You sure?"

A hum: yes, she was sure. Julia had heard them talking, and she was already planning her character's response. It surprised him in that it was so intimate, necessitating that she ask for a sip rather than simply taking one and that she snuggle up to him groggily, comfortably, her eyes half-closed and her arms still heavy with sleep. He had brought the paper with him so he could sit and read, and she took this as an invitation to lay her head on his chest. He had what many people considered a cowboy's physique: lean but hard, with big, sure hands that would rest easily on the hide of a steer. It was only the circumstances of his birth in Westchester that had kept him from the life of a ranch hand. He felt he would've been calmer on a farm, chucking bales of hay, than in that apartment, with Ewan repositioning a camera so that his naked body stretched across the frame, his genitalia in one corner and Julia's hair flaming over the thump of his heart. She was cross with him. "It's Sunday morning," she said.

He nodded. It was actually Saturday.

"Why did you have to get up so early?"

He shrugged, hoping the audience wouldn't see there was no reason beyond Weston's own discomfort. Thanks to him, Josh was no more than a naked man who hadn't wanted to sleep and who'd hoped a kindness could be exchanged for sex. That sex in that situation was possible—even likely—hadn't eluded him, and what began as jittery anticipation turned rapidly to irritation as Julia chided him about the newspaper. Her soft, hot breath was tickling over his ribs, rebuking him for his nudity as she laughed at the way he was folding and refolding the newspaper, appearing slighted. "I thought there would be something in here for us to do. You've been so busy," he said, masking his frustration. "I thought it'd be nice to go out. Have dinner, maybe see a show."

"Have I been busy?" Her cheek shifted on his chest, adjusting to the new information.

"You have."

Her hum vibrated in his ribcage, sounding like an alarm under the skin. When she asked if she'd been ignoring him, she did so sweetly—insincerely—hoping to disguise the amusement she felt in having to rest her hand on him to make him understand.

"Oh, don't do that. It'll get hard."

"Is that a problem?"

"Yes," he cried. Already the flesh was growing stiff under her hand, her fingers brushing the head as it rose slowly, assuredly. Weston had been afraid of this, of this exact moment, when his desire was masked by Josh's desire and Julia's hand was really Gwen's hand, performing acts that Julia herself would never perform. "I know you don't really want to have sex with me." He said it with his own voice, Weston's voice, breaking character to push her hand away and stand.

His response confused her. For a moment afterward, her expression wasn't Gwen's but Julia's, just Julia's: her eyes fierce, lips parted, applying herself to the problem of him with all the talent in her body. He'd dislodged her when he stood, and now she was kneeling in bed, watching him hurry around the corner. "What is it you think is happening here?"

He was already in the bathroom then. It was right next to their bedroom, its tile stretching as if down the length of a corridor so that the room was very narrow, but very long. If he had stretched his arms out from the center, he could've touched the walls with his fingers. They could hear it when he ran water on his toothbrush (a fact he'd always considered a design flaw). He understood then that he'd made a mistake, that this was not in Josh's character, and that he had to think of something fast—something that would throw the scene off balance. He found his eyes in the mirror, noting the frustration. Her hand had felt so good, like aloe on a burn. In the other room, Julia swung her legs over the edge of the bed. "Josh?"

"Leave me alone."

"I'm serious. What do you think is happening here?"

He walked into the frame, toothpaste foaming in his mouth. "You're torturing me."

"*Tor*turing you? You just turned me down." Her incredulity carried with it a faint trace of disappointment: Weston hadn't been able to think of anything better; he hadn't been able to think of anything at all. He was just standing there, waiting for Julia to take charge. He tried to convey this to her with his body language: his nervous brushing, his physical distance, his pain—not Josh's. Weston was himself for perhaps the first time since they began filming the show. She had to recognize that. She raised her eyebrows. "I put my hand on your penis. Isn't that a response?"

"Not really, no." He shook his head, confused as to why she didn't understand.

Julia sighed. "I know it's been a while," she said, rolling her eyes at the tremendous effort it required to sound sincere, but before she could finish he left the room to spit. When he returned, he was holding a towel and she was trying to convince him that she thought it was cute, his walking around like that. "Really. I wasn't trying to make fun of you."

He was at a loss. "Gwen, do you know how long it's been since we had sex?"

Julia didn't bother to hide her consternation; then she let it fade away as she tried to think of a reasonable answer—one that would explain his response. "I mean, I know it's been a while." He sighed, letting her know she had to push harder. "There was the time after Mom's funeral."

At last, he thought, slipping back into character. "That was three months ago."

Gwen opened her mouth, wondering how to respond.

"Three months, Gwen."

"I'm sorry," she said, half-amazed and half-disgusted. "It's been a difficult time."

"I know that. But you can't keep shutting me out."

That made her mad. "Shutting you out? All you want is sex."

He sighed, but she'd hit on something now: he was acting as though their relationship was falling apart because Gwen wasn't in the mood when really it had been getting better the past few months. The funeral had been, in her eyes, the first true test of their relationship and the first time Josh had been forced to step up and prove to everybody that he could hang in there when life was more than just a lovely fiancée and a silver spoon. He had been thrust into the heart of her family's grief and asked to navigate the complex network of aunts and uncles who looked at him with this tremendous sense of expectation (and, he knew, disappointment). He would have to prove he was good enough for Gwen, her mother's daughter, the last remaining piece of her legacy, and do everything in his power to honor it. They all expected him to fail, to fall back on his anxiety and his privilege and treat the wake like a war he was waging against his discomfort. Instead, he entered calmly. He shook her uncle's hand, her cousin's hand. He got her a plate when she was too distraught to do so, and at the end of the episode they sat in the back of a taxi and tears streamed down Gwen's cheeks as he held her securely in his arms. It had changed everything between their characters. It had even changed the show. In Weston's mind, that was the episode when the show went from being a mere curiosity to a full-fledged work of art destined to make a real impact. He had been so wrapped up in the gimmick of the nude performance that he'd forgotten the depths to which they'd already pushed their characters. He'd betrayed them. How could he?

"I can't believe how selfish you are. You don't care about me at all."

His mouth fell open. He said, "I do." But it was no use. Gwen was standing up, getting dressed.

He was sitting on the edge of the bed, his leg folded under him where he'd sunk, watching her wondrously, helplessly. When she threw his pants at him, telling him to put on his clothes, he let them hit his shoulder and fall to the sheet, where he blinked at them curiously before lifting his head. "I'm sorry," he said, before she ran out. "I'm sorry I walked in here naked, and I'm sorry it upset you, but you and I both know there's something wrong with this relationship. There has been for months."

He felt the truth of it hit him like an anchor in the chest: Yes, he thought. It was true. They had been drifting apart. Ever since the funeral, perhaps, or the engagement or that night they went to a club and lost each other in the music—maybe it was then. For a moment, as the strobe light surged over the jungle of bodies, he saw her—head thrown back, body swaying—and he thought, This isn't going to last. She's going to grow bored with me. And then she grew bored. Josh was doing everything in his power just to intrigue her, and the realization of this made them both immensely sad. He said, "I realize this wasn't the best way to bring up the issue . . . but I felt I had to do something. Because it doesn't seem like you're interested in fixing it."

Julia stood very still through this. There was something more she wanted to say to him, to Josh, but just then the words were swarming on her tongue, making it impossible for her to speak. That same expression was on her face—the one he saw when Julia first became Gwen and she turned to him, as if to say, Now we can begin. That's what it felt like to Weston: a new beginning.

When she opened her mouth, it was to tell him she was going for a walk and would be back later. "Do you want me to get you anything?"

"No, I'll be alright." He and Ewan would make food. They would have to do so quietly, separately, sitting alone at the kitchen table and thinking about what happened in a state of detached awe. Without saying it, they knew they had made a breakthrough. Though the camera angles hadn't been perfect and some of Gwen's dialogue would need to be rerecorded, they had filmed what was arguably the best scene in the season, the one critics would keep referring to whenever they explained its strange, human appeal. In the heat of the argument, he had somehow managed to forget that he was naked, and it didn't occur to him after to pull on shorts or cover himself with the towel.

When Julia left, he rose in a daze and went through the motions of making breakfast. He sat at the kitchen table with no pants on and only then thought of how cold it was in the apartment and how vulnerable he felt without Julia there to act alongside him. As he sat, picking at his eggs, the camera was trained on his face, watching him think through their scene. There had been a moment—just before Julia left but after they'd finished talking—when she regarded him so carefully that he felt she was trying to tell him something. Ewan would say that was the moment Gwen truly fell in love, but Weston saw it for what it was.

Her gaze betrayed no love, no longing, no hope of slow, cathartic resolution. No. She had looked at him that way because for the first time since they started performing together, Julia considered him her equal.

When it was time to call it quits, Weston invited everyone up to his cabin on Oneida Lake to celebrate the show's fifteen-year run. He and his retriever, Shep, drove up early Friday morning, arriving just as the maintenance crew came to empty the septic tank for the weekend. None of the houses on his street were connected to the sewer line and most went uninhabited during the week while the owners worked in the city. Weston was an anomaly in that he almost never went on the weekend, instead enjoying quiet evenings on the open water, where he took the paddleboat out to fish. In the six years he'd owned the cabin, Julia had visited only once, while she was pregnant, and she spent the entire time sitting on the porch, stroking a hand over her belly while Weston and her husband, Dave, grilled the hamburgers and the corn. Just once, while Dave was inside mixing the guacamole, Weston sat beside her and allowed himself to picture what it would be like to be married to her. He imagined a day just like this one, with food on the table and clouds in the sky and the sense always that there was a storm brewing, that it would drive them both inside and in time pass them. A life with Julia would not be an easy one, he knew. He had worked alongside her long enough to understand that she was guarded and to suspect that she reciprocated his affections.

There had been no discussion, no declarations. He never asked Julia to leave her husband, and she never intimated that she would. In the past fifteen years, they had shared exactly one kiss off camera: at the wrap party for a play that had been nominated for a Tony but ultimately didn't win. That it was a long kiss meant nothing, because immediately after it happened Julia disappeared with an actress, as she often did back then. Julia had been dating a woman when they started the show, and it was years before she was open to dating men again. He considered asking her out for drinks then, but they were deep into the fifth season and had already established a relationship in which he would study her, and she would let him. In the beginning, he wondered how it would feel to have eyes moving over his figure the way his did hers, and that made him self-conscious of his gaze, of its firm, demanding weight. At night, he often lay with his arms locked to his sides, afraid that the bulk of his frame would upset her somehow. Very early in the first season, he had realized the trust she had placed in him, sleeping with him week after week. And though he never touched her, there were nights when he marveled at her, at the rhythm of her breathing and the slope of her shoulders where her back was turned to him. He fell in love with her then: when she was least available to him.

He hadn't been able to sleep the night before, thinking about the weekend he would spend at the cabin. Julia had said she would stay for three days, but there was always the possibility that her husband would call or her daughter, Alma, would fall ill and she would have to leave. He tried not to think about it: those moments after filming an episode when she returned to her real life without him, never giving a thought to how it might feel to watch as she kissed Dave hello and held Alma in her arms. He kept waiting for her to slip back into character, to become the Julia he knew: the Julia who spent the week preparing for their reunion. When he heard her car pull up, it was three thirty and Shep was accosting him with a tennis ball, hoping to play fetch. He thought this might charm her, so he left Shep hanging until the very last minute, when her tires were crunching on the gravel and she was sure to see the throw. His eyes were still following the ball when he heard the engine shut off and two doors open in the driveway. Julia had brought her family.

Dave hoisted Alma from the car seat while Julia apologized for him. "His cousin lives out in Ithaca, and he thought he'd use this as an excuse to visit." She assured him it would just be for a few hours. "I figured you wouldn't mind," she said and smiled at Dave, who had wrangled Alma and her bag of toys together with his guitar and two-dozen hamburger buns. Alma was then three and a half years old and was getting too big to carry. When Dave told her to say hi to Uncle Weston, she held out her hand, as if to slap him, and he gave her a soft high five, which was what she wanted. With her fingers in her mouth, she asked if she could play with the ducky.

Weston assumed she meant Shep, who had just returned with the ball and was rubbing his chin over Julia's hip, hoping she'd play. "It's fine," he said. He was really very gentle, despite the fact that he had a death grip on the ball and growled at Julia when she tried to pry it loose. He was only playing, but still. Weston watched uncomfortably as Dave explained that she meant her rubber ducky—the one she played with during bath time. He said absentmindedly that he didn't have a bathtub, but Julia just laughed and asked if she could wash her hands.

Inside, Weston was able to regain his bearings. He stood in the kitchen mixing drinks and pitting olives while Alma toddled around the cabin. Not thirty minutes later, she was unlatching Dave's guitar case and plucking at the strings, as if trying to remember a tune. "This one's always making music," Julia said, taking up the guitar and tapping Alma on the nose. "Aren't you, my little nightingale? Can you sing a song with Mama?"

Alma's singing was sweet and enthusiastic, but she didn't fully understand the lyrics, only mouthed them with the exuberance of a child eating a peeled fruit. When she was little, Julia used to sing her songs about cherry blossoms and star fruit, and once she composed an entire song about persimmon, but if Alma understood how lovely her mother was, she didn't show it. Weston sat in awe of her, sipping a gin fizz infused with Meyer lemon and rosemary and trying to ignore the smile on Dave's face as he watched them, the two women in his life. Dave leaned over on the couch to thank Weston for doing this: hosting, he meant. "I didn't think she'd come. It's not really over for her yet, you know?"

Weston shook his head. "It'll never be over—not for any of us." After fifteen years, it was impossible to lay those characters to rest: they had grown up with them, turning thirty, then forty, facing the aging process together as their characters gained weight, went to therapy, started exercising. In the act of playing Josh, Weston had adopted some of his mannerisms and at times found himself checking his watch and scrubbing fretfully at the counter the way Josh did in earlier seasons. He felt more like himself sliding into bed with Julia than he did when he was alone, and it was in moments like that, when Julia didn't even need to look at him to be acutely aware of his presence, that he knew she felt the same way about the work.

Of course, she agreed with Dave and Weston's assessment: they became more and more like their characters each passing season. When Ewan arrived and the three principle proponents of the show were together again, Dave and Alma became outsiders, glancing curiously from person to person as if wanting to be let in on the joke.

Over dinner, they discussed the final episode of the show and what came next. Ewan was, of course, already working on his next project, a gripping character study of a woman locked in a futuristic safe house while the rest of the world destroys itself (the lead actress had been left in an old bomb shelter for three weeks to prepare for the part). Meanwhile, Dave was writing a new album to follow up his sophomore effort, and Julia was starring in a long-awaited revival of *The Cocktail Hour* on Broadway, the rehearsals for which were set to begin the following week. Weston used to feel the need to compete with Julia, to audition for parts and build a career outside television, but since buying the cabin this had become less important, and he had turned his attention instead to investing, making it possible for him to retire in his forties. Julia of course was skeptical of his decision and wondered what he would do with all his free time. When he told her—fishing—she shook her head knowingly. "It'll never work. You'll get bored."

"I haven't yet," he said, scratching Shep's ears under the table. "I like it here."

"This is a great spot," Dave said, admiring the maple trees overhead and the tiny whirling seedpod that alighted in Ewan's wine. Together they watched as the sunset feathered the clouds and the light seemed to grow wings. That was reason enough to stay, Weston thought. When was the last time he'd watched the sunset in the city? He remembered being twenty-three and sitting on the roof of a girlfriend's apartment as they drank beer and dreamed of being famous. He never imagined it would lead to this, to him thinking, It's finished. I have made my contribution. He told Julia that his agent kept sending new scripts, but none of them caught his attention. His heart was here, at the cabin. Dave could see he was in love. "You used to be so nervous," he said, drinking his wine. It took Weston a moment to realize what he meant.

Julia eyed her husband with reproach. "You've had too much."

He immediately apologized and turned to Alma to diffuse the situation. Alma, with a face like a cherub and a handful of applesauce, asked if it was time to get the ducky and was confused when he said no, they'd be going soon. With an expression equal parts wonder and consternation, she watched as her father began stirring the applesauce. "I already ate my dinner," she said, then hesitated before accepting the first spoonful. Her face crumpled. "The applesauce is dirty now."

While Julia took Alma to wash up, the men cleared the table, Dave quietly topping off his glass with the last finger of wine. He muttered to Weston, "Don't tell," then he rolled both his sleeves up to wash the dishes. Weston was actually a little pleased by Dave's outburst, because it made Weston seem mature by comparison, and that could only be a positive. But he also knew Dave was rattled and that there was no real reason to incite a confrontation, not with Julia staying the weekend. Instead, he picked up a washcloth and dried the plates, setting them on a shelf above the sink. Ewan stood to one side, fishing the seedpod out of his wineglass.

Dave cleared his throat. "So, Ewan, how do you feel about the show ending?"

He shrugged. "It's ended before." It had very nearly ended after the twelfth season, but his lawyer managed to worm out of their contracts and secure a place for them in the burgeoning online market. They had enjoyed three seasons of total creative freedom, and the entire series was now streaming on devices everywhere. This finale was merely a way for *Weekend* to reach a new generation of viewers and for Ewan to realize his vision for the show. "If it hadn't ended it would be incomplete. No one would be able to say with any certainty whether the characters had learned or that their lives were even worth watching, but it'll all be clear now," he said, lifting his glass to the word "Monday."

"Monday," Weston repeated, then had to explain the final episode to Dave: they were sleeping—Josh and Gwen—for almost the entire episode, and then, just a few minutes before the credits, their alarms went off, and Gwen laid her head on Josh's chest. "It's morning," she said in a tone of wonder and disappointment. Josh asked, "What's today?" And Gwen replied, "Monday."

Her schedule was busy, and she recited it to him even as he lay there with his eyes shut, trying to will himself to sleep.

It was always going to end that way. When the sun rose on their workweek, they became two entirely different people, and their audience realized that, as long as they'd been following their characters, they didn't really know them at all. Ewan had planned this all from the beginning. "In lieu of death, there is the dawn."

Dave passed a hand over his forehead. "I must be drunk, because I really don't get it." His laugh worried them, but Dave said he was fine, and their concern only made him more defensive, so when it came time for them to go, he cradled Alma against his shoulder and asked Julia to speak with him in the foyer, behind the bug screens. Weston made a point of opening a drawer to mask the sound of the conversation, but he knew, without having to hear, that Dave was accusing him of something, and that because of this Julia was having to defend him rationally and with no reservations regardless of what she might think or feel for him. He liked to think it was hard for her, not because Dave was upset but because her relationship with Weston predated Dave and anchored her to a life where the lines between reality and fantasy blurred and where thinking she might be in love could make it true. When she came back inside, she seemed at a loss.

Weston dried his hands on a towel. "Is everything alright?"

"Fine, thanks," she said with a small twitch of a smile. "He has an idea for a song."

Weston smiled at this, charmed by the grace with which she managed this situation. Only later would he realize that Dave was disappointed in her and in the life he had chosen. Ewan would say that Dave felt threatened by the future, perhaps because there was still so much of it. But Weston suspected this was really Ewan's tragedy and that this explained his inability to settle down. His affairs never lasted more than six months. At that time, he was dating a Swiss-German mountain climber named Inge, who called him at the cabin—perhaps to break up. When Ewan returned, he looked upset, and Julia asked him to entertain them with his Werner Herzog impression.

"The trick," he said, "is to draw the root of your tongue back into your airway and force the words to form in the back of your throat." His entire explanation was itself an impression, of course, so when he gave an example it felt as if he had rehearsed it specifically for their vacation: "The enormity of their flat brain. The enormity of their stupidity is just overwhelming." He was talking about chickens.

Weston proposed a toast to the weekend, and they lifted their glasses in celebration. It was time to get roaring drunk, and Weston kept them steadily supplied with whiskey sours and vodka tonics. In his youth he had been a bartender and spent his evenings cutting limes and wiping counters with the towel he kept on his shoulder. This was endlessly impressive to Julia, who was especially fond of the plastic swords Weston used to skewer the garnishes. After eating her cherry, she engaged both him and Ewan in a sword fight, then surrendered due to laughter. In the course of the evening they also sang songs from *The Lion King*, wrote some embarrassing texts to Inge when Ewan was in the bathroom, broke a glass thumb wrestling, and watched Shep chase his tail for a good half hour. When Julia finally stood, she was a little wobbly, yes, but she spoke with conviction: "I want to shower outside."

There was a shower stall built into the porch, right around the corner from the grill, and at midnight Weston accompanied Julia outside and lit the oil lamp to hang over the stall. In the dark of the new moon, he listened to her shower. From the porch swing, where he sat staring up at the stars, he could hear the water coursing over her, its streams gathering under her chin and between her breasts; he was able to distinguish between when she was washing her hair and when she was just standing there, and he smiled when she dropped the soap and went searching for it in the dim corners of the stall. That wood would be warm and slick to the touch, a kind of living, responsive architecture that shivered happily whenever she rested her temple against the wall. He had known that kind of pleasure: the joy of a shower you could lie down in, the wonder of staring up at the stars through a cascade of water. When she came out with the lamp in her hand and her body wrapped in a towel, her skin was glowing, and she seemed not at all drunk. "Just let me put something on," she said, then set the lamp on the picnic table before slipping into the cabin.

Weston had made the beds in the afternoon before Julia arrived. He'd given her his room, the master bedroom, and unfolded the sleeper couch in the living room, where no one would hear Ewan snore. Weston himself would sleep in the old loft, unless Julia invited him to bed with her, as he prayed she would. When Julia returned, his dark fleece comforter was wrapped around her as a cocoon, and her hair was wet and smooth where she had brushed it. "Your teeth are chattering," he said, but that didn't seem to bother her at all. Ewan was asleep, and they were alone in the cool night air.

"I find it refreshing," she said, wrapping her arms around her legs under the comforter. "It reminds me of what it felt like to be young and invincible." In her midtwenties, she said, she had gone skinny-dipping in a lake just like that one with a boy not unlike Weston—lean, talented. He had gray eyes, which she remembered. He kissed her in the moonlight, and later he invited her to join him and his girlfriend in their hotel room overlooking the lake. Without her having to say so, Weston knew that she had done it and that she had enormous respect for this young, adventurous version of herself who saw an opportunity and took it.

"You're a different person now," he said. Not sadly, only stating a fact. When she nodded, he understood that their time had passed and that the sex between them now would feel like it did in the final seasons of the show, when some subterranean desire had driven Josh to press his cheek to Gwen's stomach and then keep pressing and keep pressing until the tears started in earnest and he'd stroked himself to completion. In the ugliness afterward, she'd held his face in her hands and whispered to him with such pity, such tenderness, that when Julia turned to Weston, sometimes it was all he could see: the strain of her expectation. "Don't ask me," her silence said. "There'd be no joy in it now." When Julia stood and began slowly to descend the stairs to the docks, he couldn't help thinking that this was part of the show and that soon the cameras would be turned off so he could run after her without breaking character. Any minute now, he kept thinking, until the moment the oil lamp faded and he admitted he'd have to pretend.

Night Beast

Somnambule, I called her. Somnambule pirouetting in the night. I shivered the first time I found her pressed against me in bed, her cold, insistent fingers working their way under my shirt. My brother had told me that she was a sleepwalker, that sometimes he'd wake up in the middle of the night and have to ease Sydney down off the table or the couch because she was dancing with her eyes closed and didn't realize how close her head was to hitting the fan. He hadn't mentioned the sex or the touching, but he probably hadn't expected it to be an issue. And of course I didn't tell him. I thought it would embarrass him. He and Sydney had been dating for three years by then, and he'd started thinking about marriage. He told me in confidence that it was time to either get married or break up. He'd had enough of Sydney's empty commitments. And yet she was the one who called to invite me to the wedding.

It was on a Saturday, the third Saturday in April, at Sydney's parents' house in Connecticut. My brother had hinted on several occasions that her family was rich-rich, but I'd never met them, and I didn't think anything of it when I read the word "estate" on their wedding invitations. Sydney had merely said the ceremony would be held in her parents' backyard. She failed to mention that this yard included statues, gardens, and a little brook her parents had installed to mark where their property ended and their neighbor's began. It didn't surprise me in the slightest that they had just one neighbor, a pediatric surgeon whose father had been the governor of Connecticut. When I pulled up in front of the house, I considered turning around and skipping the wedding entirely, but then a truck drove up beside me, and someone directed me toward the garages, and I resigned myself to the fact that this was happening. She was going to marry him right in front of me.

My brother didn't answer his phone, so I walked around the estate, half expecting to learn he'd fled the country at the last minute. Someone told me that he was in the back, helping put up the big tent, but when I arrived, six men were working together to drive metal stakes deep into the grass, and my brother was gone. A tall, silver-haired man in a gray button-down shirt had taken his place, watching the men with an expression of disbelief and, it seemed, mild resentment. This was *his* backyard, I realized. *His* daughter getting married, just two months after getting engaged. When he saw me, his face went blank, and his hand slipped out of his pocket so he could shake mine. "Austin Carver. You're looking for your brother?"

I nodded. Only then did I realize that Austin wasn't wearing shoes.

"He's in the attic. Sydney wanted him to find 'something blue' for her."

Inside, I discovered that Sydney's dancer friends had arrived en masse not long before and that the pretty, limber lot of them had camped out in the living room to practice a number they'd prepared for the rehearsal dinner. When I asked if any of them knew where my brother was, a particularly flexible woman rose into an arabesque and said, very casually, as if it should be obvious, "Ruining Sydney's life." Finally, one of two piano players pointed vaguely at the stairs, and I left to search the second and third floors.

By my count, there were five guest rooms, all but one of them filled with suitcases and garment bags that Sydney's guests had brought. I had yet to encounter any of my brother's friends, whose white ties and black dress shoes would've given them away immediately. Sydney never dressed up like that unless she had to. When I found her, she was lying on her side with her back to the door, wearing a black tank top and skinny jeans. Her side rose and fell softly with her breathing, but otherwise she didn't move.

"Sorry," I heard my brother say from the attic stairs. "It's been hectic."

I nodded into the room. "Should we wake her?"

Something in him seemed to deflate when he saw her. Disappointed, he sat on the edge of the bed and touched her arm gently. "Sydney. Sydney, Gemma's here."

And indeed there I was.

Sydney rubbed her eye. "Did you find Mr. Snuffles?"

My brother shook his head. "I can look again later."

She sat up, apologizing because she hadn't meant to sleep so long. "I just had to get away from the music for a while. It was so *dreary*." She said all this to me, because I hadn't been there, but then turned to him, watching his face as she sighed. I shut the door so her guests couldn't hear it when he reminded her that it was *her* idea to have her friend's band play the wedding, that *she* was the one who'd insisted on having a less traditional ceremony, so she shouldn't complain. It wasn't my fight and didn't strike me as a particularly nasty one, so when he said he was sorry but babysitting a bunch of drunks wasn't exactly his idea of a nice wedding, I decided I didn't need to be there anymore and asked if there was someplace I might shower. I might've said it louder than necessary, because Sydney said, "Oh," then directed me toward my room. We wouldn't be sharing.

It was impossible to picture Sydney and my brother together. Their interactions only minutes before began to warp and ease apart in the steam, as if they'd happened separately, independently, joined only by the efforts of a tired mind working ceaselessly through the night. At some point I stopped moving and just stood there, letting the water cascade over me until I forgot why it was there. My first thought was that it was strange, their haste to be married. He'd only proposed in February, and he'd always wanted a big wedding, the kind you had to plan for months in advance. I knew for a fact that Sydney wasn't pregnant. When I'd last visited them at their brownstone in Brooklyn, she had come downstairs, found me in the living room, and stripped in front of the blue light of the television. She'd woken up just as she knelt between my legs and then kissed me gently, hesitantly, awake for perhaps the first time since this all started. I understood her then. I knew she didn't love him.

I stepped out of the shower, wrapping my hair in a powder blue towel. I paused a moment at the window to feel the cold air emanating from the glass. It was a dark, chilly day, and the white folds of the tent were flapping in the breeze. Its stakes had finally been secured, and the hired hands were moving tables around. Austin was there, speaking to one of the crew members. As I watched, he passed in and out of sight, first entering the frame from the right, and then exiting—still barefoot and still speaking— alone under the windowsill.

I decided to take my time getting ready for the party. Sydney had said it was going to be a casual dinner, and though I'm sure she didn't mean for me to ignore my brother's knock or spend half an hour languishing around in my bra, trying to decide whether to do without it, that was just what I did. I laid my clothes out neatly on my bed, then stood there with the sleeves of my blouse pinched between my fingers. Occasionally I flicked the sleeve around, as if enticing a shy partner onto the dance floor.

When I finally emerged, the house was quiet. I descended from the third floor in a state of waning anticipation, hearing no voices, making no introductions, only listening to the sound of my skirt rubbing against my legs. In the kitchen, I found a woman washing a dish at the sink. She wasn't thirty, but she wore the pinned-back hair and full-length skirt of someone who has longed all her life to be fifty and impossibly elegant. "Oh," she said. "You must be Gemma."

I was standing in the doorway, my hand resting on the frame. "Where is everyone?"

"Outside. You hungry?" Her hand guided me to the buffet on the counter, falling easily to the small of my back as she described each dish with exceeding care: here, flat iron steak, pan seared with a Moroccan-inspired spice rub of cumin, ginger, coriander, and clove; there, a peppery roast squash, with not just one but two salads—the first with Israeli couscous and pomegranate and the lesser with the basic arugula and balsamic. It was a little overwhelming, and when I asked if she had made it all herself, she just laughed and said her name was Olivia. "Feel free to help yourself. Hopefully some of it appeals to you."

Everyone had already eaten. They'd pulled a table up to sit in the light of the porch, and a dozen or more chairs were packed tight into a circle. Some of them were empty. A number of the guests, plus Sydney, had slipped off their shoes to go exploring in the yard—its cold, cold grass and decorated wedding arch. I could hear someone giggling inside the big tent. One of the skinnier boys was sitting on his partner's lap, resting his cheek on top of her hair. Another girl was slouched deep in her chair, a cigarette hanging idly from each hand as she gazed skyward. My brother sat stiffly in what felt like a corner, worrying a used-up wet wipe in his hand. His glass stood near the edge of the table, a single puddle of wine lingering over the dark heart of the stem. Olivia was nowhere to be seen.

At last my brother tossed the wet wipe onto his empty plate. "You're late."

I frowned at the way his foot jittered on his knee. "Are you okay?"

His shoulders jerked. Then he seemed to realize how rude that was and sat up straight. He said, "I'm fine," shaking his head. But he wasn't fine. It was like that time in high school when a girl he didn't even know smacked him in the face and he spent the entire day walking around in a huff, saying "some people" and "who does that girl think she is." I gave him the same look I had then: the "yes, but you don't have to be so ridiculous about it" look. He recognized this and I think perhaps felt stung by it, but didn't even begin to relax until Sydney returned and placed a hand on his shoulder. He shook out a sigh, then told her, "I'm ready for the night to be over." It was the most honest thing I'd ever heard him say.

With Sydney at the table the guests became suddenly animate. They were all performance artists, I realized, musicians and designers and dancers, like Sydney, who had been lucky enough (or else desperate enough) to find a way of manipulating their art into something that could make money. I watched my brother as he interacted with these people. I saw the way he coiled and drew entirely into himself, tense with anxiety and perfectly aware of his inability to join the conversation. As they spoke he nodded and hummed and occasionally said yes, but on the rare occasion when he offered something it was only an anecdote or an inconsequential fact gleaned from a news article he'd read earlier that day. When one of them made a joke, he laughed like someone who has spent their entire life trying to understand why on Earth something is funny, only to discover absurdly late that what makes the thing funny is simply that it exists. Once, he found such a thing so preposterous that he bent over with his forehead in his hand, laughing and gasping for air. The artists were all amused by this. I found it condescending.

At some point, I began to stare off into space. The porch light had illuminated a perimeter inside of which the million blades of grass stood pale and quivering, like captive animals. If only we could turn off the light, I thought, then their poor souls would have a chance to flee and in the morning we would finally see the darkness underneath.

I thought once more of the nights Sydney and I spent together, of opening my eyes and folding back the sheet to find her already there. I couldn't control her. Her tongue moved, but not in any way that would give pleasure or that was meant to give pleasure, and when I tried to draw her attention to a particular spot, either the angle would shift or the pressure abate or she'd use her teeth in a way I found dangerous and inspiring. I think part of me has always believed love should be like this—painful and hidden, only making itself known when you least expect it and are unprepared for the damage it can do. Once the pain subsided, I lay back with my eyes closed and my hands folded on my abdomen, enjoying myself. Even after I finished, Sydney continued to work on me, using broad flat strokes that pushed at my mind and almost lulled me to sleep again.

When it was over, she stretched out beside me and slipped into a deeper, less active sleep. It's amazing to think now of the calm that descended as soon as her mouth left me. As I lay there I had the experience not of dread but of knowing that something dreadful was coming and that

I'd have to be ready for it. So I got out of bed. I washed my face. Then I returned to Sydney, holding her close and stroking her hair for as long as I could before she walked out on me again.

This was the real reason I came to the wedding: because I wanted to be near her, to see her face when she was forced to choose between him and me. I wasn't expecting Olivia to flirt so much. When she emerged from the giant tent and saw me sitting there at the table, she tucked her face slightly, happily, a smile playing on her lips. She came directly to my side, taking the empty chair beside me. Her hand floated out to tap my empty plate. "Did you like the food?"

I nodded, flicking my eyes to the tent. "What were you doing in there?"

"Communing with the spirits."

"Oh? I thought you looked like a witch."

I'm not sure when exactly, but Sydney noticed that Olivia and I were casually flirting and ignoring the other guests at the table. She stared at us, not at all directly or conspicuously but still often enough for me to take pleasure in the thought that she was jealous. And so I kept talking to Olivia long after she ceased to be interesting and even after the exhaustion set in; I'd been awake, I told her, since six that morning, and I wouldn't last much longer. I brushed my hand sleepily over her arm, enjoying the tension mounting around us as the others realized what I was doing. After an hour or so, Olivia excused herself to use the restroom. "Don't disappear."

When she was gone, my brother fixed me with a look that said: What are you doing?

I soon learned what that was about, through a series of less than subtle questions posed to Sydney about a woman named Kim: where was she and was she still working that eighty-hour-a-week job and when was the last time they got to hang out with the two of them? So Olivia had a girlfriend, and everyone knew about it. My brother flashed me a helpless, almost apologetic look, as if to say he would've told me about Kim sooner had I given him the chance.

One of the women sitting near me seemed particularly ashamed of the way the exchanges about Kim were handled; she kept smiling at me in a pouty, vulnerable way, as if I'd reminded her of a time when she was in a very similar situation. She tried several times to get my attention, and when I finally allowed it she said, "You two look more alike as the night goes on."

I glanced at my brother. "Are you sure that's not just the booze talking?"

My brother and I were nothing alike physically. He was broad, fit, and angular, and he often put more care into selecting the proper belt than I did into entire ensembles. But that wasn't what she meant. "It's like you're both constantly biting your tongue."

This was true. It was part of our polite midwestern upbringing. Even when we were kids, hanging out with our friends and skipping school, there was a quiet about us, like the darkness on a clouded night. We often snuck out into the cornfield together, waiting until our mother was fast asleep, then creeping out into our backyard, where the dirt was near black with minerals. In those moments, he was as cold and vigilant as a guard dog, his gaze fixed somewhere in the distance. He would acknowledge me only through the fact of his silence and then dissolve into the cornstalks, his footfalls heavy on the loam.

Once inside the cornfield, there is no other world. Only the endless orderly rows and their unshucked ears standing taller even than your own. Sometimes the stalks will bend as if intent on hearing your innermost thoughts and feelings. Whatever you're willing to tell us, they seem to say. Whatever you're comfortable sharing. But the character of the corn can change in an instant. One minute it's as calm as a barn swallow in sleep and the next it takes flight, its heavier stalks whipping around like bats. How could you ever trust a field so fickle? I tried. In the beginning I tried. My brother walked in front of me, aiming a flashlight at the ground so it would give off as little light as possible. The point was not to see but not to fall. To instead remain as dark and quiet as life so your blood would always be your own. I didn't understand at first. I told my brother about my friend Marisa. How she fell off her bike one day and that was how it started. Just my kissing the wound to heal it—that was enough for him to pause and half turn and tell me, "That sort of thing you should keep to yourself. No one's going to understand it. Not like you do."

My immediate thought was: Oh—I should've known better. He started walking again and at a much less forgiving clip. I watched his silhouette begin to blur into the shadows and thought, Is there something I don't know about you, brother? I think if I were to ask him point-blank I wouldn't get a direct answer. He'd probably just shrug and ask me what it was I wanted to know, as if he could think of nothing worth saying, nothing in particular.

Sometimes, I resented him this ability to shut himself away, to compartmentalize all but the most necessary or inoffensive pieces of his personality, but soon enough I would come to learn his monsters by the shapes and sizes of the boxes that contained them. There was his stiffness. His reservation. His confusion when confronting the sheer nonsense of a keg party. The unabashed relief on his face when the flap of the wedding tent lifted and Sydney stepped out into the night. He held on to her there as if she were a weapon, some tiny, nimble dagger that fit perfectly into the chink in his armor, protecting him from harm. Looking at them then, they seemed perfect for each other, absolutely perfect. But Sydney's eyes found me in the dark, and the look on her face struck me like water strikes a stone.

I downed the rest of my wine in one gulp and then sat a moment, thinking how that was a mistake. Finally, I set my wineglass on the table, taking the time to press it back from the edge. I thought of apologizing to my brother but had no idea for what. Instead, I told him I was going to bed, and that would've been a clean getaway if I hadn't stumbled across Olivia in the kitchen.

She was on all fours, ineffectually sopping up a spill with a paper towel. Austin stood behind her, a dry sponge in his hand and a pained look on his face. I left them there without a second thought and slept in the next morning. I texted my brother that I was too hungover to come downstairs, then spent the morning feeling snappish and dehydrated and like I'd been made fun of. I kept thinking about that moment when Sydney glanced from me to Olivia and then back in that way, as if she'd never been so furious. I had hoped she would visit me in the night.

My brother came to check on me at quarter to eleven. "Our cousins are here."

After some consideration, I said, "You look like you're hiding."

"It's getting a little crazy out there," he admitted.

I thought he would say something more: he sat forward in his chair, then sat back; opened his mouth, then closed it. Eventually he stood up and said Sydney wanted us to come down to eat now that her father was making us brunch. It was one of his favorite things, he told me, but when we entered the kitchen, Austin seemed frantic. Not entirely out of his element, but experiencing a kind of mounting frenzy as he scuttled between the refrigerator and the stove. He kept saying okay and rubbing his hands together as he asked himself, "What next, what next?" This put my brother on edge. He started to strum his fingers on the counter and sucked in these strained, audible breaths, as if he'd forgotten how to exhale or that exhaling was a thing. When he fluffed his hair, I called him a prima donna, but all he did was open his mouth and produce the idea of a laugh with three short bursts of air.

Sydney wasn't in the room for this. She'd been with us, briefly, hovering at my elbow and trying to appear more amused by her father's antics than she really was; but she had drifted away to speak with her musician friends, who were holding an impromptu jam session in the backyard. When she returned, she tapped me on the arm, asking how I'd slept, and so began a day in which she spoke occasionally to other people, yes, but still focused the vast majority of her attention on me, asking was I hungry, would I like something more to eat, then after brunch offering to help with my makeup, my dress, wondering what was I planning to do with my hair, thinking, perhaps, that if she doted on me, I'd crack and try to talk her out of the wedding. But I wasn't my brother. If she wanted something from me, she'd have to prove it.

My brother monopolized the mirror in Sydney's room, so she got dressed in mine. We were alone then, though the door was open and people could and did flit in and out, asking if there was something they were supposed to be doing. I made my peace with that. I decided to wait until the last possible moment to slip into my dress, a simple sheath that hugged my chest and matched my hair; then, with nothing to do, I watched Sydney get ready. Her dress was beautiful, white and simple and strapless, and her shoes were perfect, but she was having some trouble with her makeup. Twice she tried applying eyeliner, and twice she had to clean away her mistake and start again. When she started shaking her mascara, I said, "You look like you're having a nervous breakdown."

"Ha." She flicked her tongue out to wet her lower lip, having never learned how to bite it. A sound like amazement escaped her as she considered what I'd said. "You're such a bitch," she said, sighing and laughing to herself as she lifted her face to the mirror. I snapped my eyes at her, but she didn't notice. She'd gone almost completely still: her mouth hanging open, her hand with the mascara in it hovering just a little to the right of her eye but never appearing to move. And then?

Then Sydney caught my eye in the mirror and giggled. I scoffed. "You're one to talk."

"I never said I was a nice girl," she shrugged. "I wasn't raised in the heartland."

"I never met any nice girls in Iowa. Everyone was a disaster."

Sydney shook her head, leaning into the mirror. "You don't cut *anybody* slack, do you?"

I didn't feel any need to answer that. I still had to fix my hair, and without direct access to the mirror there was nothing for me to do but sit on the corner of the bed and do it over Sydney's shoulder. I tried three different hairstyles, first pulling my hair up into a ponytail, then brushing it into a smooth sweep draped over my right shoulder, then braiding it on both sides so the tails met underneath one of those messy, seemingly unstructured buns my ex-girlfriend used to like. If I'd only had the forethought to bring a backless dress, then I could've just shaken my hair loose and let it tickle my shoulder blades all through the wedding. I didn't notice when Sydney finished her makeup but did pause near the end when she asked in a careful voice if I needed help. "No, I like doing it myself."

She blinked several times but didn't take her eyes off me. "I see." Then she snapped to attention, tuning in to the sounds from below, the comings and goings and discordant melodies of nothing being as you imagined it. Somehow in all of this she was able to distinguish one voice in particular. "Oh," she said, shooting me a worried look. "Olivia's here."

This didn't bother me in the slightest. "Did she make the cake, too?"

Sydney regarded me carefully and told me—again—that they were having cupcakes.

I began pinning my hair in elaborate fashion. "Cupcakes," I said aloud. I can't believe my brother agreed to that. I still can't believe it. I think back on the preparations for that wedding, on the week spent planning and the hours spent primping, and I ask myself, what was that? What even happened to me? There are vast swaths of time from which I can remember nothing in particular. Overwhelmingly, the experience of attending my brother's wedding was one of solitude and of a vague, unpleasant regret. It seemed so interminable at the time, but when I think back on it now I find only a handful of clear memories.

I try to hold them at bay as long as I can. I sit in a chair and watch my brother fiddle with his tie. I step outside but say hello to no one, only slick two fingers over the nape of my neck, the sweat that must've been gathering there for some time, though I hadn't noticed. It's warmer today. The guests are gliding back and forth between the open bar and the many spheres of conversation rolling aimlessly over the lawn. When will things begin, I wonder, and soon enough an ordained woman settles in under the snapdragons and salvia to say all the necessary words. At the moment they kiss, I'm glancing down at my heel, having momentarily lost my balance after a glass of champagne that put me over my limit. A hand steadies me. Or perhaps reaches out to me in a moment when I seem overcome. But then the touch is gone. And then the ceremony's over. I have been told that I'm wanted for wedding pictures, though I'm not sure where. My brother and Sydney have ducked behind the tent to get a few shots of them alone, and they take so long to get them just so that I drift off toward the buffet. Sydney has to come grab me. She says, "Silly, where were you? We've been waiting." And for the first time I feel grateful to her for the attentiveness she's shown me all day; without her I wouldn't know how to behave. "Smile," she whispers, and we pull ourselves together long enough to at least seem like a family. But I wonder what we'll look like when everyone's gone and there's no need to pretend.

The reception lasts deep into the night. I realize my brother wasn't kidding when he said these people don't practice moderation. The three of us sit together and entertain a rotating group of guests, each of whom asks them how it feels to be married, and, each time, my brother glances at me as if it's a joke (all of it, the wedding, the cupcakes), as if to say, Can you believe it? Every so often someone asks, "Was he like this when you were kids?" And because I'm drunk I call him my bastard older brother and say I can't live without him like it's the sweetest thing in the world.

When no one's paying attention, I tend to space out. I stare at Sydney's wedding ring. Sometimes I see Olivia carrying dishes back and forth between the kitchen and the tent and I wonder if she'll take a turn sitting with us, or if she's avoiding our table because of me. Her girlfriend's beautiful. Kim. They're sitting together a few tables away and look happy enough.

I dance alone. I don't give a shit what anyone thinks. The music here's good, surprisingly good, and I move the way I like. I keep dancing until my hair shakes loose of its messy bun, until Olivia has gone and taken the threat of her indiscretion with her. By now, the dancing's devolved into a kind of slow-motion pulse in which bodies seem not to move so much as vibrate in concert with their partners. Up until now, Austin has been dancing somewhat awkwardly with a group of Sydney's friends who've accepted him somehow as the cool dad they always wanted, but when the grinding starts in earnest he becomes extremely uncomfortable and excuses himself.

He doesn't bother to tell Sydney. She's too engrossed. She and my brother are moving so gently they seem almost to be standing still. She has her back to him. Her hands press against his thighs. His eyes are closed, and as I watch she lifts a hand to his cheek and drags her nails under his ear. Something in his response or his lack of one makes her sigh and gaze out over the dance floor.

She must stare at me a full minute before making eye contact.

I touch her arm and shout, "Are you leaving?"

"Yeah. He's already asleep." She pats his cheek roughly, repeatedly.

His eyes open to a slit. He yawns, "Is it time?"

"You bet it is. You can barely stand up, mister." She gives him a hard little peck of a kiss and pats his cheek again, slapping him until he lays his hand over hers, and somehow even this is a sign of affection as they lean hard into each other, content in their drunkenness. It occurs to me: I've never seen her relaxed before. Something shifts in between us (either in the way I look at her or in how much she enjoys it), because she regards me with a beatific smile; she offers her hands, and when I take them, she peels away from him, asking, "Are you done?" And some other words I don't hear but I'm sure qualify the question. "Promise me you'll stay the night."

"Oh—is that all?"

This is funny to her. She laughs my name—Gemma, Gemma—as she extends her arms.

"I'm so sweaty," I warn her, but she hugs me all the same.

The party dissolves quickly then. The musicians pack up, the dance floor clears. Sydney's father stands on the porch, directing those too drunk to drive inside so they can sleep it off on his living room floor. I drape myself over a chair and feel the crowd part around me. I can hear them go, their voices receding, their cars starting, but I don't bother to watch it happen. I have my eyes closed and I'm focusing all my senses on my feet as I drag them through the lush late-night grass. It doesn't frighten me now. The blades are harmless and wet; the yard is empty and I don't know where I left my shoes. I try to think: When did I take them off? It takes long minutes to retrace my steps to that exact moment. I still don't remember it, really. All I know is: one minute I was up, ambling through the sea of chairs, and the next the back door had slammed and sent my heart racing for safety.

Sydney. She was coming down the stairs.

Her hands danced in the air, her arms swaying like a professional that's planning to fake a fall in front of their audience. I knew that she'd seen me, and that's what made me hesitate when I heard my name on her lips. She began to twist, her shoulders moving in ways I didn't understand while she held one hand remarkably, alarmingly still; when I took it, her dance started to change, adopting a muted character, as if we were riding out a low, quiet wave.

I was able to look Sydney in the eye then. She was asleep, I realized. Her eyes were wide open and her body was animated, but she was gone—off in some distant dreamland that undulated like the sea. They must've fallen asleep as soon as they got upstairs. Sydney hadn't even managed to take off all her clothes—her wedding dress, modest thing that it was, was riding up her thighs.

How long did we dance? Certainly for longer than was decent.

Eventually, my brother came looking for her. He was still wearing his white shirt and polished shoes, but his suit jacket was missing and he'd already removed his belt. His pants were sagging as he stepped out on the porch. His face looked as though it had been scrubbed of the possibility of happiness. He said her name softly, plaintively, in a tone I'd never heard before and never heard again. Perhaps he was sleepwalking too, I thought. Perhaps we were all sleepwalking and this was just some dark and frightful dream that our minds had conjured to distract us as they sorted through our hearts under the protective blanket of night.

He'd been silent for so long that I jumped when he snapped at Sydney to wake up. He strode toward us, catching her right arm with a surprisingly gentle touch, as if he were merely changing the direction of a balloon. It took some coaxing to bring her back. "Syd. Syd. You were at it again."

She turned her face to his. "Was I? That's not good."

His hand came to rest on her cheek. He considered her for a long time (her blue eye shadow, her naked shoulders, her slim, graceful figure), as if prepared to let her go if that was what she wanted. He kissed her on the forehead and then asked, very quietly and very pointedly, if she wanted to keep dancing. I knew even before she shook her head that it was over. That she'd chosen my brother. He'd woken her up in a way I never could. He turned to me then, turned so he and Sydney were both facing me, as if to show me who she really was and what she really meant to him. Her sleepy eyes. Her sorrowful dances. He wanted me to see. Underneath all the exhaustion and the betrayal, I found the silence we'd shared as kids—that deep, reverberating hollow sounding like the cannons of a grim and distant victory. He said nothing then, only pulled Sydney inside. I stood for a long time after, staring into the emptiness of the door through which they disappeared. It was cold then, and the leaves were rustling with the breeze. I shut my eyes, listening to the night—its great and inimitable roar.

ACKNOWLEDGMENTS

First and foremost, I want to thank my mentors: Lan Samantha Chang, Stephanie Vaughn, and Alice Fulton. Their guidance, support, and feedback have been crucial to my development as a writer, and I quite literally don't know where I'd be without them. I would also like to thank my teachers at Iowa: Benjamin Percy, Ayana Mathis, Kevin Brockmeier, Julie Orringer, and Marilynne Robinson, for the time and energy they put into workshop. And Connie Brothers, Deb West, and Jan Zenisek, for keeping the workshop running.

Special thanks go to Debbie Kennedy, first reader and friend extraordinaire. Rebekah Frumkin, friend and confidante. My friends and classmates from Cornell and Iowa, particularly Susannah Shive, Renée Branum, Amy Parker, JT Keller, Yaa Gyasi, Alexia Arthurs, Kyle Minor, Mason Scisco, Anna Noyes, Tea Obreht, Ezra Dan Feldman, Laurel Lathrop, Elizabeth Lindsey Rogers, and E. J. Fischer, for their time and support.

ACKNOWLEDGMENTS

I'm grateful to the readers and editors who picked these stories out of the slush pile: David Lynn, Sam Martone, Allegra Hyde, Kim Winternheimer, Ryan Ridge, Ander Monson, Lydia Millet, and Megan Giddings. And the contest judges who did the same: Mary Gaitskill and Kelly Link, two of my writing idols.

To Ross Harris, Nicole Nyhan, and Amy Hundley, whose enthusiasm and support made this book possible.